JIM ELDRIDGE

WRESTLING TROLLS

MATCH 4

THUD IN TROUBLE

ED
4/15

Illustrated by JAN BIELECKI

HOT
KEY
BOOKS

First published in Great Britain in 2015 by Hot Key Books
Northburgh House, 10 Northburgh Street, London EC1V 0AT

A CIP catalogue record for this book is available from the British Library.

ISBN: 978-1-4714-0265-4

1

This book is typeset in 14pt Sabon using Atomik ePublisher

Printed and bound by Clays Ltd, St Ives Plc

www.hotkeybooks.com

Hot Key Books is part of the Bonnier Publishing Group
www.bonnierpublishing.com

ALSO BY JIM ELDRIDGE

Contents

THUD IN TROUBLE

CHAPTER 1

The ancient, battered caravan with the letters WWT (Waldo's Wrestling Trolls) on the side trundled along the country road through the long valley, pulled by the old horse, Robin. It was a beautiful sunny day, not a cloud in the sky. To one side of the road a gentle stream flowed, and now and then there was a *plop!* as a fish leapt to catch a fly, and then disappeared beneath the surface of the water again. The sound of crickets and other small insects in the short grass could be heard, chattering and buzzing. Above all these sounds came that of Milo and Jack, singing cheerfully in time to the clip-clop of the old horse's hooves.

'Wrestling Trolls.
Tum-di-dum!
Wrestling Trolls.
Tum-di-dum!'

Big Rock, the Wrestling Troll, ran beside the caravan as it rolled along, every now and then doing a little hop into the air. Above them flew Blaze the Phoenix, making patterns in the sky as he flew, and every now and then changing shape into different flying creatures – a dragon, a butterfly, an eagle – before turning back into a phoenix.

> 'Wrestling Trolls.
> Tum-di-dum –'

'Do you have to keep singing that song?' complained Robin. 'It's just the same words over and over again and it's driving me mad!'

'All right, how about this one?' said Milo. And he broke into:

> 'Wrestling Trolls.
> Toot-a-toot!
> Wrestling Trolls.
> Toot-a-toot!'

'Yes, I like that one!' said Jack, and he joined in:

> 'Wrestling Trolls.
> Toot-a-toot!'

The caravan jolted to a halt.

'Stop!' Robin said. 'That's the same song!'

'Nearly,' admitted Milo. 'But it's got "Toot-a-toot" in it instead of "Tum-di-dum".'

'Well, I'm not moving another hoof until you agree to stop singing.'

'Actually, we don't need to go any further,' said Milo. 'We're here.'

'Where?' asked Big Rock, running to join them.

Milo pointed towards a cluster of houses and other buildings, which they could just see through the trees.

'That's the town of Rampot where the Wrestling Challenge is taking place.' He smiled. 'Twelve gold coins to the winners! And you, Big Rock, will collect that money on our behalf when you beat Buster Gutt, the Rampot Heavyweight Champion! This is a good place to park the caravan.'

'All right, but no more singing,' grumbled Robin.

'We only sing because we're happy,' said Jack. 'Why don't you join in?'

'Because I'm out of breath from pulling this heavy caravan.'

'Don't worry, you can rest now,' said Milo, unhitching him.

'I ought to go into town and get some food and stuff,' said Jack. 'We're running low.'

'Good idea,' said Milo. 'You can check out Big Rock's opposition while you're there, this Buster Gutt. I've never seen him wrestle, but I hear he's good.'

'I'll go with Jack,' said Blaze, spreading his wings. 'I can turn into a dragon and give him a lift back with the shopping.'

'Toilet rolls,' said Big Rock. 'Need toilet rolls.'

'Leave it to me,' said Jack.

While Milo, Big Rock and Robin made camp, Jack set off for the town, with Blaze flying just above him.

Rampot was a very old town with narrow streets packed with old houses. Most of the buildings looked to be made of wood, but a few were half wood and half bricks. Jack and Blaze stood and surveyed the town. It was busy, packed with shoppers hurrying to and fro, loaded down with bags and baskets.

'I'm glad we parked the caravan where we did,' said Jack, looking at the narrow streets that twisted and turned in a maze. 'We'd never have got it through the town. We'd have got stuck.'

'That never seems to bother Robin,' commented Blaze. 'He just plods on regardless.'

'Yes, then we have to get us out of the trouble afterwards,' said Jack.

'I think I see a general store down there,' said Blaze, gesturing at one of the streets. 'Hopefully, that'll have everything we want.'

'That depends on the prices,' said Jack ruefully.

He hoped things would be cheap here because – as always seemed to be the case with the gang – they were very short of money. That was why they'd come to Rampot – for Big Rock to win enough money by taking on Buster Gutt for them to be able to eat and make necessary repairs to the caravan, including fixing its roof, which let in the rain.

They walked down the street to the store. Jack was just about to walk in when he found his way blocked by a large man. No, more than large – this man was enormous: tall, with a large belly and huge muscular arms.

'What are you doing standing in my way?' growled the man.

'I'm sorry, I didn't realise I was in your way,' said Jack, and he went to go round the man.

The man scowled and moved to block Jack from going into the shop, but as he did so he trod on a little puppy, which squealed with pain.

'Careful! You hurt Bobby!' cried a little girl, and she snatched up the puppy and began to cuddle and stroke it.

'Don't you *dare* tell me to be careful!' shouted the man. 'I'll show you what I think of your stupid little dog!'

And with that he snatched the puppy from the little girl and drew back his arm as if he was about to throw it.

'No!' appealed the little girl desperately.

Anger welled up in Jack as he saw the big bully squeeze the little puppy in his huge fist, making it whimper.

Before Jack knew what was happening he felt the change come over him as rage poured through his body; a glassy film formed over his eyes and he felt himself growing outwards and upwards, getting massive . . . becoming Thud the Giant Wrestling Troll.

'*GRAAARRR!*'

The roar that came out of his mouth made the enormous man turn and look at him in surprise. Before the bewildered bully could react, Thud had taken the puppy from the bully's grasp with one hand and gently passed it back to the little girl, while his other hand had bunched into a fist and thudded forward, thumping the bully so hard it sent him flying backwards, crashing into the door behind him with such force that it was torn off its hinges. There was the sound of pots and pans falling down inside the shop, and then a shopkeeper ran out, a look of shock on his face.

He pointed his finger accusingly at Thud and shouted, 'You! You did that!'

The dazed figure of the bully staggered out of the shop, a large dented saucepan crunched down on his head. One of his eyes was already swelling up into a large purple bruise, and as he opened his mouth one of his teeth fell out.

'You broke my door and wrecked my shop!' carried on the shopkeeper.

'He saved my puppy, Mr Brown,' the little girl appealed to him.

'That may be, but it'll cost a lot of money to get my door mended! Money I can't afford!'

At that moment, the bully, still stumbling around in a dazed state, fell over, crashing to the ground with a dull thud.

'Ow,' he groaned.

'Guards!' shouted the shopkeeper. 'Guards!'

CHAPTER 2

Milo was lighting a fire so that they could cook a meal once Jack arrived back with the ingredients. Big Rock was munching on a few pebbles he'd found, and Robin was grazing on the grass. Milo looked at the others eating, and his stomach rumbled. It seemed like a long time since he'd had a hot meal.

'Jack and Blaze are taking their time,' he said.

'I expect he's haggling with the shop owner,' said Robin. 'After all, you didn't give him very much money.'

'We haven't got very much money,' pointed out Milo.

The sound of wings flapping made them look up.

'Jack's been arrested!' said Blaze, landing beside them.

'What! Why?' demanded the shocked Milo.

'He turned into Thud and punched a bully who was threatening a little girl and her puppy.'

'Good Jack,' nodded Big Rock approvingly. 'Help weak people.'

'It's not good when he gets arrested!' retorted Milo.

'Trouble, always trouble!' complained Robin. 'Every time that boy turns into his troll side –'

'He usually does something good,' countered Milo. 'Although it doesn't sound like it this time,' he added unhappily. He turned to Blaze. 'Where is he now?'

'The guards took him to the cells in the guard station. He's going to appear in court today.'

'Right, we'd better get over there and save him,' said Milo. 'Robin, can you stay here and look after the caravan while we go in?'

'I always get the hard jobs,' grumbled Robin.

* * *

Jack sat on the hard wooden bench in the cell. He felt bad. Milo had been telling him for ages that he ought to learn to control when and where he turned into Thud, and he'd tried but failed. Now here he was, locked in a cell.

A heavy metal door connected the cell block with the guard station. The cell itself was bare. It had three walls of brick and stone, with a tiny barred window, set high up in one of the walls, that looked out onto the street. The window was too high off the ground for Jack to be able to see out of it, but he could hear noises coming from outside: people muttering in low voices.

The fourth wall of the cell was made of metal bars, with a barred door in it. To Jack it seemed to be more of a cage than a cell.

It was very secure. Even Thud wouldn't be able to punch his way through those metal bars, thought Jack.

There was the sound of a key turning in the lock of the connecting door, then it swung open and a guard came into the cell block,

with two more behind him, armed with spears and swords.

'Right! You . . .' began the first guard. Then he stopped. He looked around the cell, bafflement on his face. He turned back to Jack and said, 'Where is he? The big troll?'

'He . . . er . . . he's not here,' said Jack.

It was a difficult situation. Jack turning into Thud was a secret. They'd all agreed that it would be best to keep it quiet until Jack was able to control his transformations better.

The guard looked even more baffled. He walked over to the outside wall, looking up at the high barred window. Then he turned back to Jack again.

'How did he get out?' he asked. Then, even more puzzled, he demanded, 'How did you get in here?'

'He must be a friend of that big troll,' said one of the other guards. 'I bet he snuck in to help him escape, and somehow the troll got out and left this one behind.'

'Is that what happened?' snapped the guard

at Jack. 'Are you and that troll friends?'

'Yes,' admitted Jack.

'Right,' said the guard grimly. 'Well, the Judge isn't going to like this! You are in big trouble!'

CHAPTER 3

Jack stood in the dock at the court, where the prisoners on trial were put. Immediately behind Jack stood a guard, with two more standing on either side of the small boy to make sure he didn't escape. They were obviously treating Jack as a very dangerous criminal.

The story about how the bully had been bashed and knocked into the shop must have spread all over town, because the courtroom was packed with people eager to see more of this person with the devastating punch. Every seat was taken and there were loads of people standing, crammed into every available space in the courtroom.

The building itself was very old – dark

wooden panels covered the walls and ceiling. On the wall behind the large gold chair where the Judge sat was a huge shield with a coat of arms: a pair of crossed swords and above them a very large ram with giant horns coming out of its head, standing with its four hooves on top of what looked like a big flowerpot. The word RAMPOT was painted in gold letters on the shield.

Jack was so small that he could barely see over the edge of the dock. He wondered where Milo was. He hoped he'd be here to try and save him.

'What is your name?' demanded the Judge.

'Jack, sir.'

'And what is this person, Jack, charged with?' the Judge asked the guard.

'Er . . . that's a difficult one, your Judgeship. The charge was assault, and causing damage to a shop.'

'Assault?' echoed the Judge. 'Who was assaulted?'

'Buster Gutt, your Judgeship.'

The Judge's mouth dropped open in astonishment.

'Buster Gutt, the Champion Wrestler?' He stared at Jack in bewilderment. 'Are you telling me that this . . . puny little boy . . . assaulted Buster Gutt?'

'Well . . . not exactly, sir . . .' said the guard awkwardly.

'Is Buster Gutt here?' barked the Judge.

'He's outside, sir, waiting to give evidence.'

'Bring him in!'

A court usher went out, and returned a moment later with Buster Gutt. So this was the wrestler Big Rock came to battle, thought Jack.

The big bully had a black eye and looked very unhappy. The Judge ordered Gutt into the witness stand, and then said, 'Were you assaulted recently?'

'I was, your Judgeship,' said Buster Gutt. 'I was punched and knocked through the door of a shop.'

'It was my shop!' called a voice from the back of the court, as the shopkeeper stood up. 'It's going to cost me a lot of money. There's a new door to replace the broken one, and lots of pots and pans and things were dented and broken.'

'Thank you,' nodded the Judge. 'You may sit down.' He turned back to Buster Gutt. 'Who punched you?'

'A big troll.' Gutt scowled. 'He caught me off-guard with a sneaky punch, otherwise I would have beaten him easily.'

The Judge pointed at the frail figure of Jack in the dock.

'Is that the person who assaulted you?'

'No!' said Gutt indignantly. 'I could eat him for breakfast. Like I said, it was this huge and sneaky troll!'

The Judge turned to the guard.

'Then why is this troll not here in court instead of this . . . small boy?' he demanded.

'Because this boy helped the troll escape from

the cell,' replied the guard. 'He's an accomplice.'

'Very well.' The Judge glared at Jack, and then announced, 'I hereby fine you two gold pieces for assault, and order you to pay a further eight gold pieces for the repairs to the door and the shop.'

'But I haven't got any money, your Judgeship!' protested Jack.

'In that case you will stay in the cell in the guard station until someone else pays your fine for you.' Turning to the court, he asked, 'Does anyone here know this boy?'

'Yes, your Judgeship!'

Jack turned and saw that Milo and Big Rock had just entered the court.

'Who are you?' asked the Judge.

'My name is Milo and I am the manager of Waldo's Wrestling Trolls. This is Big Rock, one of my wrestlers.'

'Hello,' smiled Big Rock.

'Jack there is our assistant trainer.'

'Do I take it that this mysterious troll who assaulted Buster Gutt is also one of your Wrestling Trolls?'

'He didn't actually assault him, your Judgeship. Buster Gutt was threatening a little girl and her puppy, and Thud – that's his name – intervened to try and save the puppy from being hurt.'

'He hit Buster Gutt?'

'Yes, your Judgeship,' admitted Milo.

'Then he's guilty. Right, if you hand over ten gold pieces –'

'Actually, your Judgeship, we haven't got any money. That's the reason we came here, to enter the Wrestling Challenge and win the prize money. It's twelve gold coins if someone beats Buster Gutt.' Milo grinned. 'And, as Thud *did* beat Buster Gutt, we ought to get the twelve gold coins now, and then we can pay you.'

'He didn't beat me!' protested Gutt. 'It was a sneaky punch when I wasn't looking!'

The Judge glared at Milo.

'I order you to bring that big troll, Thud, here so he can be locked up until the fine is paid!' he snapped.

'Er, I'm afraid he's gone, your Judgeship,' said Milo miserably.

'In that case, I order this boy, Jack, to be locked up in his place until the fine is paid. Next case!'

As the guards hustled Jack away, down to the cells, Milo and Big Rock hurried to him.

'Don't worry, Jack, we'll get you out of this!' Milo promised.

CHAPTER 4

As Milo and Big Rock left the court, they found Buster Gutt waiting for them in the street. With him was a crowd of his cronies, all smirking or scowling threateningly at them. Buster Gutt and his pals blocked their path to stop them from moving.

'So your Wrestling Troll has run away from me, hey?' smirked Buster Gutt.

'He didn't run away, he just had . . . something important to do,' said Milo awkwardly.

'More important than wrestling me?' jeered Gutt. 'He's a coward! He knows I'm the best wrestler there is, so he ran away!'

Big Rock shook his head angrily.

'Thud no coward,' he said. 'He beat you.

I beat you. Robin our horse beat you!'

'Oh yeah?' snapped Gutt. 'Well, put your horse into a ring with me and see who wins!'

'Actually, horses aren't allowed to wrestle,' Milo pointed out. 'But Big Rock here is. So, how about it?'

Buster Gutt took a look at Big Rock, and hesitated.

'Well . . .' he began doubtfully.

He's not going to go for it, Milo realised. And if he doesn't wrestle Big Rock, we've got no chance of getting the money to get Jack out of the cell.

By now a crowd had gathered around them, curious to find out what all this arguing was about.

'You're scared!' said Milo accusingly. 'You know that Big Rock can beat you!'

'Rubbish!' called someone from the crowd, and others – all obviously Buster Gutt's friends and cronies – joined in. 'Buster Gutt can beat that big lump of stone, easy!'

'Okay, then. It's a challenge,' said Milo. 'You against Big Rock.'

Once more Buster Gutt hesitated, but as the shouts from his supporters grew, with cries of 'Yeah! Go for it, Buster!' and 'Show the big troll!', Gutt nodded.

'Okay,' he said. 'Me and him. My manager, Murky, will be in touch to sort out the details.' And he stabbed a finger at Big Rock. 'I'm gonna make pebbles out of you, Troll. You are gonna be in big *rubble*!'

And with a laugh at his own joke, Gutt stomped off, with his friends and cronies following him, cheering.

'You hear of manager called Murky?' asked Big Rock.

'Yes.' Milo nodded. 'He's sneaky and a crook. Not to be trusted. I bet he and Buster Gutt try something nasty.'

'Not easy winning here if they cheat,' said Big Rock thoughtfully.

'No, it isn't,' agreed Milo. 'It might be best if we forget about wrestling Buster Gutt and move on.'

'Can't,' said Big Rock. 'Jack in cell. I beat

Buster Gutt for money to get Jack out.'

'Yes,' said Milo. Then he smiled. 'Unless there's another way.'

'There no other way,' said Big Rock.

Milo smiled even more.

'Actually, Big Rock, there might be. I have a plan.'

CHAPTER 5

Jack sat on the bench in the cell. He felt miserable. There was no way he could see himself getting out of here, unless Big Rock beat Buster Gutt. Although Jack was very confident in Big Rock's skills and was sure the troll could beat the big bully, there was something very nasty about Buster Gutt. Jack was sure that Gutt would come up with some sneaky way to cheat a victory.

'Hello.'

Jack heard a tiny little voice, and was surprised to see the face of a small girl looking at him through the bars. It was the little girl whose puppy Jack had saved.

Jack got up from the bench and came to the door.

'How did you get in?' he asked.

'My mum mends the guards' uniforms,' she said. 'I was bringing one to the guard on duty, and he let me in for a few minutes. My name's Sally. I know yours is Jack because I saw you in court.' She frowned. 'How did you turn yourself into that big troll?'

'That wasn't me,' said Jack quickly. 'That was my friend, who just turned up.'

'It was you,' said Sally. 'I watched you change when you saved my puppy.'

Jack hesitated. He could try and pretend she'd imagined it, but she looked to be a genuinely nice sort of person, and he hated lying to nice people.

'I'll tell you if you promise not to tell anyone else,' he said. 'It's a secret.'

'I promise,' said Sally.

'It's because I'm a half-troll,' said Jack. 'It sometimes happens when I get angry, or see something bad happening. Like that bully about to hurt your puppy.'

'Can't you turn into him now? Then you'd

be strong enough to break out of here.'

'I can't control it,' admitted Jack unhappily.

'I wish I could help you,' said the girl. 'The trouble is, the bully you hit . . .'

'Buster Gutt,' nodded Jack.

'Yes. Well, he's so tough and terrifying that everyone is frightened of him. That's why people cheer him when he wrestles, because they're frightened of him.'

'That's how bullies work,' said Jack, sadly. 'I know about being bullied. It happened to me when I worked in the kitchens of Lord Veto.'

'Lord Veto? The rich man who runs Lord Veto's Wrestling Orcs and the other sports stars?'

'That's him,' said Jack. 'He was horrible. He bullied me, and everyone who worked for him. But finally there came a day when I stood up to him and told him I wasn't afraid of him any more. And since then, he hasn't been able to bully me. He's tried, but it doesn't work on me now.'

Sally sighed gloomily.

'That's all very well for you,' she said. 'But standing up to Buster won't work. When people tried it, he bashed them.'

'They should have reported him to the guards and the Judge. They would have stopped him.'

Once more, Sally sighed.

'The people in charge of this town are Buster's family. They own nearly everything here. And they're all bullies.'

Jack frowned thoughtfully.

'When things are bad like that, sometimes

you have to come up with a *clever* way of stopping them.'

'How?'

'Well, bullies get away with it because everyone thinks they are tough and frightening. But if you try and see a bully in a different way – like, imagine him sitting on the toilet, or with no clothes on – you see they're just the same as ordinary people. And if you can maybe make them look silly in some way, then they won't be frightening.'

A sound from the corridor made them both look round.

'The guard's coming!' said Sally.

She stepped back from the door, and Jack saw a guard appear, followed by Milo and Robin. The guard unlocked the cell door.

'Right,' he said. 'You can go.'

'What?' asked Jack, bewildered. 'Why?'

'Because I'm taking your place,' said Robin, and the old horse clip-clopped into the cell.

'I told the Judge we needed you as assistant trainer for the wrestling match,' explained Milo.

'So he agreed that Robin could be held here as a kind of hostage.'

'But if you don't come back, this horse will never be let out!' snapped the guard.

'Oh, I think I'll be all right,' said Robin. And, to Jack's surprise, the old horse gave him a wink.

As Jack, Milo and Sally left the guard station, Jack asked, 'What's going on? Why did Robin give me that wink?'

Milo cast a look at Sally, and then said quickly, 'I'll tell you later.'

'I'd better go home,' said Sally. 'My mum will be wondering where I've got to. Thank you for saving my puppy from Buster Gutt, Jack. I hope your friend beats him wrestling, so you can all go home.'

With that, Sally hurried off.

'What's so secret that you won't tell me?' asked Jack.

'I couldn't, not in front of that girl.'

'I think she can be trusted,' said Jack. 'She saw me change from Jack into Thud, and she hasn't told anyone.'

'Hmm.' Milo frowned. 'All right, maybe she can be trusted with some things. But not this one. This one is special.' And he winked at Jack.

'What's with all this winking?' demanded Jack. 'First Robin did it, now you.'

'You'll find out when we get back to the caravan!'

CHAPTER 6

As Jack and Milo neared the caravan, Jack saw Big Rock hurry towards them – a huge smile on his face and his big arms held out in greeting.

'Jack!' he said. 'You back! Good!'

And the giant troll scooped Jack up and hugged him, being careful not to hug too hard.

As Big Rock put him back down on the ground, Jack was stunned to see Robin walk into sight from behind the caravan.

'Robin?' Jack said, bewildered.

'Hello again,' said the horse. 'Good to see you out of jail.'

'But . . . but . . .' stammered Jack. 'I left you in the cell!'

'Not exactly,' smiled Milo. 'You left Blaze in the cell.'

'Blaze!' Jack exclaimed. Now he knew what the winking was for. Of course! Blaze was a phoenix, able to change shape and become other animals!

'The plan is that once we leave here, we pass the guard station and signal to him. He'll turn into a small bird, fly out between the bars of the window and we all head off. Brilliant, eh?'

Jack stared at Milo and Robin, stunned. Then

he shook his head. 'No,' he said. 'We can't.'

'Can't what?'

'Sneak off like that.'

'Why not?' demanded Milo. 'This way we all get away safely.'

'Yes, but Buster Gutt will have won. This all started because of his bullying. If we sneak off people will think that Big Rock was too scared to wrestle him, and that will only make him even more of a bully.'

'Good point.' Big Rock nodded. 'Need to beat Buster Gutt in ring, show everyone. Make people stop feel afraid of bully.'

'Exactly,' said Jack.

'No!' exploded Milo. 'That's madness! We have to get away safely, while we still can. It's nothing to do with us if people are afraid of Buster Gutt. This isn't our town!'

'It's everybody's business,' said Jack. 'People like Buster Gutt start by being a bully in their own street. Then they spread out and bully the district, then the town. Next thing, they move on to other places and start bullying them as well. Once they get to that stage, no one can stop them. Bullies have to be stopped before they start.'

'Jack's right,' said Robin.

'Yes,' said Big Rock, nodding again. 'I go in ring, beat Buster Gutt. We get money. We pay fine. We go home.'

'My way's quicker,' insisted Milo.

'But it's not right,' said Jack.

Milo groaned.

'So I suppose I'd better go back to the guard station and tell Blaze he can come out.'

'No,' said Robin firmly. 'If he does, it means I'll have to go in, now we're staying, and a tiny prison cell's no place for an old horse like me. Blaze is younger than me, and he can change into comfortable shapes, like a mouse. He won't mind being in the cell.' Then he looked hopefully at Jack. 'We know Thud can beat Buster Gutt . . .'

Jack gave a heavy sigh. 'I've tried and tried, but I can't control it.'

'Maybe if we got that little girl here with her puppy, and I threatened it?' suggested Milo.

'That's what happened before.'

'Yes, but I'd know you were pretending. It won't work.'

'No problem,' said Big Rock. He thumped his chest with one of his enormous hands. 'Big Rock beat Buster Gutt. I win and we be okay.'

CHAPTER 7

Jack and Milo found the back of the guard station and saw the one barred window high up on the wall.

'That's it,' said Jack.

They looked along the narrow street, making sure that no one was watching them, then Jack climbed onto Milo's shoulders. He grabbed hold of the bars of the cell and pulled himself up so he could look through.

'Pssst!' he called.

Robin the horse (or rather, Blaze the Phoenix) looked up and smiled.

'There you are!' he said. 'Good! Now I can get out of this shape and fly off!'

'Not quite,' said Jack.

Quickly, he explained the change of plan. 'I'm sorry,' he apologised. 'It's my fault. I was the one who said we couldn't go yet. It was a good plan – but I want to stay here and show people they needn't be afraid of Buster Gutt.'

'I thought it must be something like that when you didn't come back straight away,' said Blaze. 'Still, I don't mind. It's just that it's not easy keeping a different shape for a long time.' With that, the figure of Robin the horse shook its mane and burst into flames, to be replaced by Blaze the Phoenix.

'You'd better not stay like that,' warned Jack anxiously. 'The guards will work out what's going on.'

'Don't worry,' said Blaze. 'Every now and then I change back into myself. When I hear the door opening and someone coming, I turn back into Robin. It's very tiring, but if me staying here helps, I don't mind.' The phoenix frowned anxiously. 'Do you think Big Rock can beat Buster Gutt?'

'We hope so,' said Jack.

'But I'm worried that Buster Gutt will cheat in some way,' said Milo, from where he was standing beneath the window. 'He's a bully and his manager, Murky, is a known cheat. They're bound to try something.'

'In that case you'd better get back to the caravan and make sure that Big Rock's okay,' said Blaze.

'Robin will look after him,' said Milo confidently. 'He's a wise old horse.'

'He's also very shaggy and heavy,' complained Blaze. 'The sooner I can turn back into myself and stay that way, the better.'

'It'll just be until after the wrestling match has finished,' said Jack.

'Hey!' shouted a voice.

The boys looked round and saw a guard glaring at them.

'What do you think you're doing? Get away from there! That's a dangerous prisoner!'

'Sorry,' said Jack, getting down from Milo's shoulders.

As they walked away, they heard Blaze

chuckle. 'A dangerous prisoner! Wow! Robin is getting quite a reputation.'

Jack and Milo had reached the edge of town and were about to cross the field to their caravan, when they heard Sally's voice calling urgently to them, 'Stop! Wait!'

They turned and saw that Sally was running fast towards them, with a small boy next to her. The two children reached them, both out of breath.

'Ben says . . .' Sally began, panting, then stopped and tried again. 'Ben says . . .'

'Calm down. Wait until you've got your breath back,' urged Jack.

Sally nodded. She took a deep breath, then burst out, 'This is my friend, Ben Brown. His dad's the owner of the shop where Buster Gutt got bashed up by your friend.'

'Ha!' snorted Milo angrily, glaring at the boy. 'In that case, we don't want anything to do with you. It was your dad that put Ja— Thud in jail. And he gave evidence against him in court!'

'That's because he's afraid of Buster Gutt,' said Ben. 'My dad's not a mean man, just frightened, like everyone else in this town. Right now he's feeling bad about your friend being in jail.'

'Ben overheard something bad,' said Sally. 'You've got to listen to him!'

'I overheard Buster Gutt telling one of his pals about a plan his manager, Murky, has come up with to make sure he beats Big Rock,' said Ben.

'What is it?' asked Milo.

'Murky has laced some sweet pebbles with a poison that will affect Big Rock's eyes. If he eats them he won't be able to see for a whole day!'

'We were just coming to your caravan to see you and tell you,' said Sally.

'Oh no!' said Jack, shocked. 'We have to warn Big Rock!' He broke into a run towards the caravan, with Milo, Sally and Ben following close behind.

Jack could see Big Rock in the distance, and

there was someone else walking away from the caravan towards them. As they got nearer, they saw it was a man. He smiled as they approached him.

'Well, well!' He grinned. 'You must be Milo and Jack. My name's Murky. I thought I'd make a courtesy visit to you and your wrestler before the match, just to be friendly, like.'

'What have you given Big Rock?' demanded Jack angrily.

Murky's smile grew even bigger. 'Just some sweets,' he said. And he winked. 'You know, a friendly gesture.'

And with that he laughed and walked past them, heading back to town.

Jack felt anger rising in him and he stretched out an arm to grab hold of Murky, but then his anger faded.

'We have to stop Big Rock eating those sweets!' he shouted, and he began to run again, with Milo, Sally and Ben racing as fast as they could behind him.

CHAPTER 8

'Big Rock!' yelled Jack as they neared the caravan. 'Stop eating!'

'Stop eating what?' asked the big troll, looking up at them in surprise from the steps of the caravan.

Jack, Milo, Sally and Ben skidded to a halt, and saw that Big Rock had a handful of small pebbles in the palm of his hand.

'Have you eaten any of those?' asked Milo urgently.

'Only couple.'

'Ha!' snorted Robin, appearing from inside the caravan. 'I've been watching him. He's been stuffing them down like he's never had sweets before! I warned him they'd rot his teeth . . .'

'They'll also make him go blind,' said Jack.

'*What?*' said Robin. He looked at the sweets in Big Rock's hand. 'What are they?'

'Poisoned,' said Milo, 'with something that will stop Big Rock from being able to see for hours.'

'Just in time for him to be in the ring with Buster Gutt,' added Jack bitterly.

'But he nice man!' protested Big Rock. 'Said he come to give me a present.'

'I told you he wasn't to be trusted,' snorted Robin. 'I've told you before, never take sweets from a stranger!'

'Why didn't you stop him?' Milo demanded of the old horse.

'Because I'm not supposed to be here! I'm supposed to be in a cell,' Robin reminded him. 'I hid in the caravan.'

Ben and Sally exchanged puzzled looks.

'Yes,' said Ben. 'I thought your horse was in jail?'

'It's a long story,' said Jack. 'We'll tell you about it later.'

Suddenly Big Rock let out a cry of alarm. 'Fog over eyes!' he said. 'Me can't see!'

'It's happened already!' groaned Milo.

'What are we going to do?'

'Me can't see!' repeated Big Rock nervously, and he stood up and took a step forward and then tripped over and fell to the ground with a crash.

'Stay down, Big Rock!' ordered Milo. 'You can sit up, but don't try and go anywhere. Robin, you stay here and look after Big Rock while me and Jack go and see the Judge to ask him if we can put the match with Buster Gutt off until tomorrow, when Big Rock will have his sight back.'

'Maybe Ben and I can come up with something,' said Sally thoughtfully.

'What can *you* come up with?' demanded Milo.

'I don't know, just at this moment,' said Sally, 'but I'm sure we can think of an idea if the Judge doesn't let you put the match off. We'll see you later.'

With that, Sally and Ben hurried off towards the town.

'Nice kids,' said Robin.

'Yes, but I can't see what they can do to help if we can't persuade the Judge,' sighed Milo.

'They may surprise us,' said Jack, looking after Sally.

'Yes, but they may not,' snorted Robin. 'In which case, Milo, you'd better make sure you persuade the Judge.'

CHAPTER 9

The Judge sat behind his desk and listened as Milo and Jack made their appeal for the match to be put off until the next day.

'And you say that the fact that this Wrestling Troll, Big Rock, can't see is because Murky, Buster Gutt's manager, gave him poisoned sweets that made him lose his sight?'

'Yes, your Judgeship,' said Jack. 'We don't know exactly how many hours he'll be blind for, but he should be all right tomorrow.'

'That is outrageous!' said the Judge, angrily.

'Indeed it is, Judge,' said Milo. 'But that's the sort of sneaky person Murky is. Not to be trusted!'

'I am talking about your unfounded and

false allegation against someone who is an old friend of mine,' snapped the Judge. 'Murky is a highly respected member of the Rampot Town Council! How dare you!'

Taken aback, Milo and Jack stared at the Judge.

'Then you won't put off the match until tomorrow?'

'Absolutely not!' stormed the Judge. 'This is obviously some trick of yours to get out of paying the fine. I've given you the chance for your troll to battle Buster Gutt for the prize money. If he doesn't win and you can't pay the fine, then I shall keep your horse in prison until the Town Council can sell it to get the money for the fine. And, because I think you're the kind of people who are obviously sneaky and tricksy, I'm going to insist the guards are at the match today to make sure you don't sneak off if your troll loses! If he does, I shall have the lot of you arrested. Now get out!'

Jack and Milo trudged away from the Judge's building, feeling gloomy.

'We'll have to make a run for it now,' said Milo. 'Once we're at the wrestling match, we won't be able to.'

'Big Rock won't do that,' said Jack. 'You heard what he said – he wants to fight Buster Gutt and beat him. If he runs away, Buster Gutt will call him a coward. And it'll ruin his reputation as a wrestler. No one will want to book a coward for wrestling matches. It'll be the end of Waldo's Wrestling Trolls.'

Milo sighed heavily.

'What if Big Rock goes into that ring with Buster Gutt and loses?' he asked.

'He'll still have his reputation as a brave wrestler,' said Jack.

'But with no money, and we'll all be in a jail cell!'

'Perhaps Sally and Ben will come up with an idea,' said Jack hopefully.

'Huh!' snorted Milo. 'If *we* can't come up with anything, what makes you think they will?'

They got back to the caravan and found Big

Rock standing up. Robin rushed at him, bumped into the troll and knocked him over, and then retreated, only to rush at Big Rock again as soon as the troll had got back to his feet, knocking him over again.

'What are you two doing?' demanded Milo, horrified. 'Robin, why on earth are you bashing into Big Rock? And Big Rock – I told you to stay sitting down! That way you won't fall over and get hurt.'

'Me listen,' said Big Rock. 'Me hear sound of hooves come near, then me dodge out of way.'

'Big Rock reckons he's got a plan!' said Robin, shaking his head in disapproval.

'Me listen for when Buster Gutt makes noises and me grab him,' nodded Big Rock proudly.

'Like you did just then when Robin charged at you?' commented Milo sarcastically.

'Five times,' said the old horse, almost too triumphantly.

'That different. Robin run on soft grass. No noise. Buster Gutt make noise on canvas in ring.'

'You hope!' sighed Jack. 'Oh well, if you're going to do this, Big Rock, we'd better go. The wrestling match is due to start in half an hour.'

'I go!' said Big Rock.

And he stepped forward, tripped over a stone, and fell over.

CHAPTER 10

The Wrestling Hall in Rampot was packed, and everyone there seemed to be pals or supporters of Buster Gutt, judging by the placards that were being waved from the crowd: *Buster Gutt Rules!* and *Buster the Best!*

Jack led Big Rock by the hand down the aisle from the dressing room, walking slowly so as not to make the big troll stumble. He noticed that guards had been stationed at all the exit doors. The Judge had carried out his threat. There was no way they were going to escape from here.

'Buster Gutt!' shouted the crowd. 'Buster Gutt!'

He was already in the ring, strutting around,

waving and smiling at the cheering crowd. His manager, Murky, stood just below the ring, by Buster's corner. He grinned as he watched Milo and Jack guide Big Rock's hands to the ropes and then helped the big troll climb into the ring.

'Having problems?' asked Murky.

'Please, Jack, turn into Thud and hit him!' whispered Milo.

Jack scowled at Murky, then turned his attention to Big Rock. The big troll held onto the top rope with one hand and waved, unseeing, at the crowd with the other. As the crowd booed Jack felt anger rising in him, but not enough to make him turn into Thud.

'This crowd love Buster,' said Murky, and Jack became aware that Buster's manager had sidled over to stand uncomfortably close to him and Milo. 'See that costume he's wearing?'

They looked at Buster Gutt's costume. It looked like any ordinary wrestling costume: a leotard in bright blue with different coloured spangles on it.

'Yes?' grunted Milo. 'What about it?'

'That was a present sent to Buster,' smirked Murky. 'It came with a card that said, *Wear this today. It will bring you good luck. From an anonymous admirer.* That's how much people in this town love Buster Gutt. They give him presents all the time: teddy bears, cuddly toys . . .'

'What about poisoned sweets?' snapped Jack.

Murky shrugged. 'We were just doing a kind and friendly act, giving Buster's opponent a present of some nice pebbles. How was I to know your troll would have an allergic reaction to them?'

With that, he chuckled and walked away to Buster's corner.

'The rotten, sneaky . . .' growled Jack.

'You sure that doesn't make you angry enough to turn into Thud?' asked Milo hopefully.

Jack shook his head. 'Sorry, Milo.'

They looked up at the ring, where Big Rock was standing in his corner, holding onto the ropes, staring at . . . nothing.

'Ladies and gentlemen!' announced the referee, standing in the centre of the ring. 'Welcome to the Heavyweight Challenge Match between our very own Rampot Champion Wrestler, Buster Gutt . . .!'

Once again, the crowd began to cheer and wave their placards and chant Buster Gutt's name loudly. The referee's voice could barely be heard above the chanting as he continued, 'And the challenger, the Wrestling Troll, Big Rock!'

'Hurray for Big Rock!' yelled Jack, but his voice was lost in the cheering and chanting of Buster Gutt's name.

'Let the contest begin!'

The bell went for the start of the bout, and Buster Gutt strode towards Big Rock, who had moved away from the ropes and was standing, head cocked to one side, listening.

Buster Gutt put a leg behind Big Rock's, and then pushed him, tripping the troll, who landed on his back on the canvas. Immediately, Buster Gutt threw himself on Big Rock, using all his

weight to hold Big Rock's shoulders down for
a pinfall.

'One!' shouted the referee. 'Two!'

One of Big Rock's hands shot up in the air,
lifting his shoulder clear of the canvas. Big Rock
threw Gutt off and rolled clear, but as he tried
to push himself to his feet, Gutt charged him
and hit Big Rock full in the back, sending him
crashing head first into the corner post and
tumbling down. Once again, Gutt leapt on the
fallen troll, and this time pinned him down as
the referee counted, 'One! Two! Three!'

The crowd went wild, cheering and stamping.

'This is going to be a nightmare!' groaned Milo as the referee ordered Buster Gutt back to his corner while Big Rock pushed himself back to his feet, his hands searching to find the top rope.

'Keep stretching your arm, Big Rock!' called Jack. 'The rope's just there!'

Big Rock pushed his arm out further and felt the top rope, his hand closing over it.

'We ought to stop it,' said Milo. 'It's not fair to put Big Rock through this. I'm going to throw in the towel.'

And Milo took the small towel from around his neck and was just about to throw it in the ring as the sign of surrender, when Jack stopped him.

'No, wait!' he said. 'Something's happening!'

'You're turning into Thud?' asked Milo hopefully.

'No – something's happening to Buster Gutt!'

CHAPTER 11

'Ow!'

Buster Gutt was wincing and wriggling in his corner, tugging at his costume.

'Ow!' he said again.

He began to dance around the ring, jumping and hopping and wiggling as if there was some sort of small animal moving around inside his costume.

Big Rock cocked his head to one side.

'He's listening,' whispered Jack to Milo. 'He can hear Buster Gutt moaning!'

As Buster Gutt jumped around the ring, Big Rock suddenly stepped into his path and grabbed him with both of his strong arms and upended him, driving him head first into the canvas. As Buster Gutt collapsed, upside down, Big Rock fell on him.

'One! Two! Three!' called the referee.

Big Rock pushed himself to his feet.

'Here, Big Rock!' called Jack. 'Follow my voice!'

He kept calling as Big Rock made his way towards him in his corner.

Buster Gutt scrambled to his feet.

'That wasn't fair!' he protested. Again, he whimpered 'Ow!' and began to jump around the ring, pulling at his costume.

'Ow!' someone in the audience called out, laughing as Gutt carried on jumping around, yelping, 'Ow! Ow!'

'Ow! Ow!' mimicked the audience, and the laughter spread.

Then Buster Gutt began to roll around on the canvas and scratch at himself through his costume.

'What's happening?' asked Milo, astonished.

'I think there's something wriggling around inside his costume,' Jack whispered back.

'But how?' asked Milo.

Jack smiled.

'I think maybe the person who gave it to him as a mystery present doesn't like him as much as Murky thinks they do,' he said. 'The point is, it's causing him to make noises. Every time he goes "Ow!" or starts scratching, Big Rock can work out where he is.' He smiled. 'Like now.'

Buster Gutt had leapt to his feet and was hopping from one foot to the other again, shouting out 'Ow! Ow!' which was echoed by the crowd, who were jumping about themselves now, copying him and laughing openly at Buster Gutt's antics.

Big Rock stepped towards the yelping Buster Gutt, then stopped and listened, his head cocked to one side, to establish where Gutt was. Big Rock reached out and grabbed one of Gutt's arms and, in one swift move, flipped Gutt up into the air, and then brought him crashing down onto the canvas.

Flop!

Once again, Big Rock dropped onto Buster Gutt, who struggled frantically, his feet and legs writhing and kicking as he tried to push the troll off him, but Big Rock kept him down, shoulders flat on the canvas, as the referee counted: 'One! Two! Three! And the winner, by two pinfalls, is . . . Big Rock!'

Jack and Milo helped Big Rock down from the ring and then led him by the hand to the dressing room. As the big troll made his way out of the arena, the crowd cheered, slapping him on the back in congratulations and calling his name: 'Big Rock! Big Rock!'

A loud roar of laughter made Jack take a look back at the ring, where he saw Buster Gutt trying to pull off his costume while Murky fought to make him keep it on, ushering him away from the ring towards the privacy of the dressing room.

'Fantastic!' beamed Milo as they reached Big Rock's dressing room and went inside. 'You beat him, Big Rock! You beat Buster Gutt and that cheat of a manager, Murky.'

'Trolls got good hearing,' nodded Big Rock.

'I think it would be a good idea if you went and collected our winnings,' suggested Jack to Milo. 'Just in case Murky lodges a protest about the result.'

Milo opened the door to go, and then stopped.

'We've got a visitor,' he said.

It was Sally, and in her arms was her little puppy.

'Come in,' said Jack. 'I'm afraid Milo's got to go. Urgent business.'

'I'll see you later,' said Milo.

Sally came in and went up to Big Rock and touched his arm.

'Are you all right, Big Rock?' she asked anxiously.

'Fine,' said Big Rock. 'Eyes get better. Me see shapes.' He bent down and peered at the little puppy. 'Me see little dog.' And the giant troll

put out a hand and gently stroked the tiny puppy's head. In response, the puppy put out its tongue and licked Big Rock's hand.

'Tickles!' laughed Big Rock.

Jack looked at Sally and gave her a wink. 'It was you who fixed that costume, wasn't it?'

'Me and Ben,' said Sally. 'With a lot of help from my mum.'

'Yes, I remember you said your mum mended clothes,' said Jack.

'It was what you said about making the bully look silly,' said Sally. 'I remembered this material Mum had that got all rough and prickly when it got wet. And I guessed that once Buster Gutt started wrestling he'd get all sweaty.'

'So you got your mum to make a costume for him using that stuff.'

'Even better than that,' laughed Sally. 'To make sure it worked, me and Ben went out and collected loads of stinging nettles and we threaded them into the costume. And once Buster Gutt started sweating . . .'

'It was like he was being stung.'

'And everyone started laughing at him as he jumped around, and then Big Rock could hear where he was.' Jack chuckled. 'Thank you, Sally.'

'Yes,' said Big Rock. He patted the little girl's hand very gently. 'You beat bully.'

CHAPTER 12

The sight of Jack, Milo, Big Rock, Robin and Blaze walking into his shop made Mr Brown, the shopkeeper, look worried.

'If you've come here to cause trouble, it won't do you any good. We're not scared of bullies in this town any more,' Mr Brown snapped at them, and Jack saw that he had picked up a long-handled broom as a weapon, just in case.

'We're not here to cause trouble,' said Milo. 'We're here to apologise for the mess our friend made of your shop, and to pay for the damage.'

Milo took out his purse and counted eight gold coins into the shopkeeper's hand.

'Why . . . thank you,' said Mr Brown. 'I must

admit, I never thought I'd get paid.'

'We always pay our debts,' said Milo. 'But Thud didn't damage your shop on purpose.'

'I know,' said Mr Brown. He looked around to check that no one was within earshot, then said, 'But in a way, I'm glad he did. If he hadn't punched Buster Gutt right through my door, the whole business of the way that bully terrorised this town would never have been sorted out. So, will you thank him for me?'

'We will,' said Jack. 'And we've also come here to say thank you to your son, Ben.'

'Ben?' said Mr Brown in surprise. 'Why?'

'Because, without him, Big Rock would never have beaten Buster Gutt in the wrestling ring. And you'd all still be frightened of him.'

'What did my Ben do?' asked Mr Brown, intrigued.

'Sting nettles,' said Big Rock. 'He pick sting nettles.'

'Yes.' Mr Brown nodded. 'He picks them to make soup with.'

'Tickly soup!' laughed Big Rock.

'What's going on, Dad?' Ben asked as he came into the shop.

'These folk say they've come to say thank you to you,' said Mr Brown.

Just then two women came into the shop.

'Ah, Mr Brown,' said one. 'You look like you're busy. We'll come back later.'

'No, no, ladies,' said Milo quickly. 'We're just leaving.'

'Let's talk outside,' Jack whispered to Ben.

The gang and Ben left the shop, while the two ladies began placing their orders with Mr Brown. 'We'll need saucepans,' Jack heard one of them say. 'And frying pans.' Then the other added, 'And a whisk, Dorothy. And spoons.'

Ben pulled the door shut and joined the gang on the pavement.

'Thanks for not saying anything to my dad,' said Ben.

'Big Rock started to,' said Robin. 'He started talking about you picking nettles, but luckily your dad thought he meant for soup.'

'I like nettle soup,' said Ben.

'You still ought to tell him,' said Milo. 'He'd be proud of what you did.'

'Yes and no,' said Ben. 'He might be proud. But my dad worries a lot, so he might worry that I'd get into trouble with Buster Gutt. Even though Buster Gutt's left the town and gone far away.'

'Bullies can have that effect,' said Jack. 'Even after they've gone, some people still remember what they were like and worry they might come back.'

'Buster Gutt won't come back, not after everyone laughed at him the way they did,' said Ben. 'His bullying days are over here in Rampot.' He grinned. 'That was brilliant the way you beat him in the ring, Big Rock.'

'He couldn't have done it without you and Sally,' said Milo.

Ben grinned proudly at that. Then he asked, 'Did I hear right? You gave my dad the money to mend the shop?'

'Yes,' said Jack. 'It was the right thing to do.'

'Well, if you ever come back to Rampot, you'll

always have a welcome here,' said Ben. He smiled. 'I'll make some nettle soup for you.'

Hauled by Robin, with Milo and Jack sitting in the driving seat, the ancient, battered caravan rolled along the valley road away from Rampot, trundling beside the gentle stream.

Now and then they heard a *plop!* as a fish leapt to catch a fly, and then disappeared beneath the surface of the water again. The sound of crickets and other small insects in the short grass could still be heard, chattering and buzzing.

Big Rock, his sight now back to normal, ran round and round the caravan as it moved along, causing Robin to snort angrily, 'Do you have to keep running round the caravan like that, Big Rock? You're making me dizzy!'

'Sorry,' said Big Rock. And he stopped and then started running round the moving caravan in the other direction.

'That's just the same!' roared Robin.

'No it not,' said Big Rock. 'I go other way to unwind you and you not be dizzy.'

Above them, Blaze made patterns in the sky as he flew, every now and then changing shape into different flying creatures – a dragon, a butterfly, an eagle – before turning back into a phoenix.

'We did it,' smiled Milo. 'We got out of Rampot, and with two gold pieces' profit. And we helped make a bully look like an idiot.'

Jack nodded.

'And we did it all without you having to turn into Thud!' said Milo. He gave Jack a serious look. 'You've got to learn to control it, you know, Jack. This turning into Thud.'

'I will,' he promised. 'But right now, I just want to enjoy what we've done. With a song.'

And he began to sing:

> 'Wrestling Trolls.
> Toot-a-toot!
> Wrestling Trolls.
> Toot-a-toot!'

And soon Milo, Big Rock, Blaze and even Robin were joining in as they trundled on their way.

VETO'S REVENGE

CHAPTER 1

'Masked Avenger! Masked Avenger!'

The supporting shouts echoed through the Wrestling Hall as Princess Ava, in her Masked Avenger outfit, moved warily around the ring with her eyes locked on her opponent, Grime the Orc.

'Grime! Grime!' and 'Orcs for ever!' shouted Grime's supporters.

Big Rock, Jack, Milo and Meenu – Ava's costume-maker – stood by the ring and yelled their encouragement.

'Come on, Masked Avenger!' shouted Jack.

So far the contest was a draw: one pinfall each. A knockout or a pinfall would decide it.

As was often the case with orcs, Grime had

tried every cheating way to beat the Masked Avenger, using her claws and her sharp beak as well as her wrestling skills. And Grime's wrestling skills were good. But orcs, as Big Rock had often pointed out, didn't wrestle fair.

Suddenly, Grime dived for the Masked Avenger, aiming the point of her beak at her. As the Masked Avenger dodged to one side, Grime suddenly changed direction, and brought both her claws down hard in a slashing movement, aiming to rake them down the

Masked Avenger's body. But the Masked Avenger had sensed the orc's move coming, and her claws just hit empty air as the Avenger rolled away. Grime's claws thudded into the hard edge of the ring . . . and stuck.

The crowd went wild as Grime heaved at her claws, struggling to get them out of the wood. But before Grime could release herself, the Masked Avenger had grabbed the orc and pulled her feet through the ropes so that Grime was hanging upside down, trapped. The Masked Avenger kicked Grime's claws free from the wood, and then pulled the ropes back into the ring, hauling on them with all her strength, like the string of a bow.

'Shoot!' yelled the Masked Avenger's supporters.

The Masked Avenger drew the ropes back as far as they would go, and then released.

TWWWANGGGG!

Like an arrow shot from a bow, Grime was hurled out towards the audience. People yelled and scattered as the orc flew through the air and then crashed down onto the second row.

Grime leapt up from where she'd landed, but found her claws and beak were caught in the seats. As she struggled to free herself, the referee was counting.

'One. Two. Three. Four . . .'

In desperation, Grime picked up the block of four empty seats that had got caught on one of her claws and began to drag them towards the ring.

'Five. Six. Seven. Eight . . .'

The orc got as far as the ring, but she couldn't reach up to the ropes and climb back into it with the seats hanging off her.

'Nine. Ten! Out!' counted the referee, and the crowd erupted in cheers from the Masked Avenger's supporters and boos from Grime's.

The Masked Avenger came down from the ring to join her friends.

'That was spectacular!' said Meenu.

'Firing her like an arrow,' chuckled Milo. 'Brilliant!'

'At one point I thought she was going to get your mask off,' said Jack.

'Not a chance!' said the Masked Avenger.

So far, the Masked Avenger was unbeaten in the ring and had been able to keep her mask on. Only her close friends knew that she was really Princess Ava, teenage ruler of the country of Weevil.

As the gang trooped to the dressing room, they were watched by the angry figure of Lord Veto.

'That Masked Avenger beat my best female orc!' he snarled.

'The Masked Avenger's good, my Lord,' nodded Warg, his Chief Orc.

'I don't want her "good"!' stormed Veto. 'I want her beaten! Who is she, anyway?'

'No one knows, my Lord,' said Warg. 'She says her true identity will only be revealed if she loses in the ring. If that happens, then her victorious opponent can take off her mask.'

'Rubbish!' snapped Veto. 'Someone knows who she is. Someone must be around when she takes her mask off after a match.' And then a sly smile spread across his face. 'Like me, for example!'

'My Lord?' asked Warg.

'Hurry up, Warg! We're going to go round to the window outside the dressing rooms and look in. We'll soon find out who she is!'

WRESTLING TROLLS

FUN & GAMES

Grab paper, pens, a friend
and complete the wrestling challenges!

WRITE YOUR OWN
WRESTLING TROLLS SONG

The WWT gang love to sing a good song on their way to the next tournament, so have a go at writing a new one for them! You can change the words, or the rhythm, and make up any tune you want - just make sure it's about trolls and wrestling!

☐ I'VE DONE THIS!

'WRESTLING TROLLS.
TUM-DI-DUM!
WRESTLING TROLLS.
TUM-DI-DUM!'

ROUND 2
WRESTLING COSTUMES

Big Rock needs a new wrestling outfit (even though he doesn't want one ...) so grab some paper and crayons and design him the best costume ever! You could even create new ones for Buster Gutt and the Masked Avenger too. Make them as bright and scary as you want, but each one should be completely different - all wrestlers are unique!

☐ I'VE DONE THIS!

How well do you know the Wrestling Trolls gang? Can you spot all 10 differences between these two pictures?

DOUBLE TAKE

ROUND 3

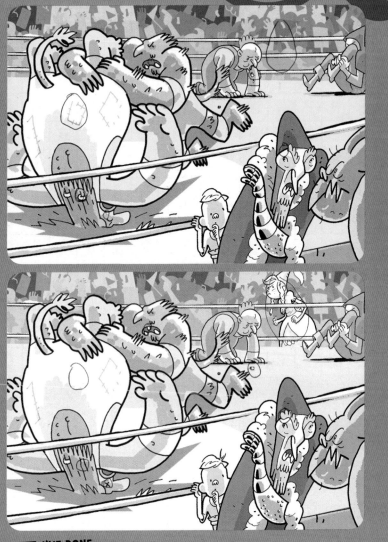

☐ I'VE DONE THIS!

1) Princess Ava. 2) The man's tooth is on the floor. 3) There's an extra rope in the top image. 4) Veto's eyebrows have grown! 5) . . . And his glove has shrunk. 6) Jack has a sticking-out bit of hair. 7) Big Rock's costume is missing a patch. 8) . . . He's also missing a ring in his hair. 9) . . . And his eyes look different. 10) Mudd the Troll has an extra tooth.

WALDO'S WRESTLING WORD SEARCH

F	W	E	D	U	D	Y	T	S	Z	A	X	C	P
H	R	R	J	M	U	O	L	J	H	G	R	B	I
B	E	T	E	T	H	W	K	T	Y	H	J	M	N
F	G	A	G	S	T	U	T	C	C	P	S	F	F
E	N	P	K	W	T	J	G	I	O	C	V	B	A
R	E	R	U	P	I	L	V	C	R	R	O	P	L
U	V	Z	C	O	W	D	I	O	E	R	G	Y	L
O	A	T	R	O	L	L	S	N	A	V	C	I	R
P	D	N	T	K	O	C	Q	I	G	I	K	M	B
L	E	A	S	L	C	E	L	B	M	U	R	T	P
K	K	B	U	S	T	E	R	G	U	T	T	J	I
Q	S	U	E	T	E	R	U	I	S	A	Q	U	A
E	A	K	R	U	N	W	O	D	M	A	L	S	D
Z	M	V	C	M	B	C	Y	O	L	P	G	H	D

BUSTER GUTT **ORCS**
PINFALL **BIG ROCK**
THUD **TROLLS**
SLAMDOWN **RUMBLE**
WRESTLING

See if you can find all 10 words on the list hidden in the grid. Don't forget to look down and up, left and right, and diagonally!

☐ **I'VE DONE THIS!**

NEW WRESTLING NAME GENERATOR

A	DREADED
B	GREAT
C	THUNDERING
D	RAGING
E	GRIM
F	WAILING
G	HORRIBLE
H	FEARSOME
I	UNBEATABLE
J	TERRIBLE
K	AWESOME
L	SHRIEKING
M	FLAMING
N	INVINCIBLE
O	MAD
P	GIANT
Q	INVISIBLE
R	MONSTROUS
S	CLOAKED
T	BRAWLING
U	MYSTERIOUS
V	DYNAMITE
W	STOMPING
X	MIGHTY
Y	DASTARDLY
Z	SMASHING

☐ I'VE DONE THIS!

JANUARY	HULK
FEBRUARY	CRUSADER
MARCH	BONE CRUSHER
APRIL	THUNDERBOLT
MAY	WHIP
JUNE	BRUISER
JULY	NEMESIS
AUGUST	THUNK
SEPTEMBER	WARRIOR
OCTOBER	MASTER
NOVEMBER	INFERNO
DECEMBER	TWISTER

If you're going to be a great wrestler, you'll need a great wrestling name, just like the Masked Avenger. Use the first letter of your name and your birthday month to work out your wrestling title!

MY WRESTLING NAME

THE _____

_____

TROLL THEATRE

YOU WILL NEED: Tracing paper, stiff card, scissors, crayons — and maybe even a friend to play with!

Re-enact your favourite scenes — or create some new ones! — with your very own Wrestling Trolls theatre.

1. Lay tracing paper over the templates and trace each one with a pencil.

2. Place your tracing paper drawing-side down on a stiff piece of card and trace over your lines to transfer them.

3. Cut out each card template.

4. Colour in your characters.

5. Fold back along the dotted line at the bottom so that they can stand up.

6. Now for the backdrop! Take a long rectangular piece of card, draw and colour in your chosen background - perhaps a wrestling ring or Princess Ava's castle? - then fold the card lengthways into three panels so that it will stand up on its own.

7. Let the troll play begin!

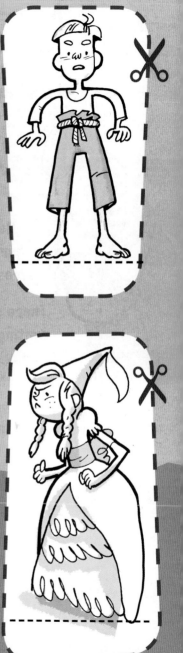

I'VE DONE THIS!

WRESTLING RING

Had fun with these games and want more Wrestling Trolls action?

There's more fun and games waiting for you right now on www.wrestlingtrolls.com with challenges, activities to download and more facts about your favourite characters!

Join the Wrestling Ring and get a free finger puppet of Big Rock to battle with. Plus, upload your creations from this section and you can also earn yourself other exclusive treats.

Log on now to
www.wrestlingtrolls.com

CHAPTER 2

Princess Ava, still wearing her Masked Avenger costume, led the others into the dressing room, where they found Robin the horse and Blaze the Phoenix waiting for them.

'Well done! You won!' said Robin with a smile.

'You saw it?' asked Princess Ava.

'No,' said Robin, shaking his head. 'They wouldn't allow animals into the audience. It's blatant discrimination!' Then he gave a grin. 'But luckily they didn't spot a very small mouse.'

And Blaze transformed himself into a tiny grey mouse, and then back into his normal phoenix shape. 'I kept Robin aware of what was happening in the ring,' he said.

'I'd still have preferred to watch it myself,' grumbled the old horse.

'I'm glad you're okay after that match with Grime,' Milo said to Ava. 'You've got another bout coming up in an hour.'

'Me and Masked Avenger against two of Lord Veto's orcs,' beamed Big Rock. 'Be good wrestling!'

'Yes – but you're asking a bit much of yourself,' said Milo to Princess Ava, concerned. 'One match in a day would have been enough, surely.'

Princess Ava shook her head. 'I need to raise some money fast,' she said. 'Weevil was hit by a big storm a week ago, which did a huge amount of damage. Homes wrecked. Gardens and woods destroyed. It's going to take money to repair the mess.'

'How much?' asked Jack.

'About a hundred gold coins,' said Ava. 'Maybe more. It could be as much as a hundred and ten gold coins. That's why I'm wrestling a lot more, to raise money for the work.'

'We beat orcs, I give my winnings,' said Big Rock.

'No, that wouldn't be fair,' said Ava. 'You need money to get yourself a new costume.'

'I like this costume.'

'But it's got lots of holes in it!' said Meenu.

'I like this costume,' insisted Big Rock stubbornly.

'Whatever we can raise at this tournament, we'll help you,' said Milo. 'That's what friends are for.'

Meenu looked at Jack and said, 'It's a pity you can't control when you turn into Thud, Jack. You and Big Rock would make a great Wrestling Troll Tag Team.'

'And how!' Ava nodded enthusiastically. 'That would be great!'

'That's what I've told him,' said Milo.

'Actually,' Jack smiled, 'I did it the other day.'

The others stared at him.

'You did? You were able to make yourself turn into Thud?' asked Milo, awed.

'Well, only for a bit,' admitted Jack.

'And without getting angry?' asked Meenu.
Jack nodded. 'I tried to *think* angry,' he said.
'Think angry?' said Big Rock, puzzled.
'I've never heard such rubbish!' snorted Robin.

'No, it makes sense,' said Ava. 'If Jack can *think* himself angry, then it ought to work.'

'Let's see,' said Milo.

'Okay,' said Jack. 'Watch me.'

He adopted a stance with his shoulders leaning forward, his fists bunched, and a scowl

on his face. Then he let out a growl.

The others stood and watched and waited . . . and waited. Jack still looked exactly the same.

'You Thud yet?' asked Big Rock.

'Nothing's happening,' said Milo.

'Give him a chance!' urged Meenu.

Jack scowled more, and this time he let out a roar.

Again, the others waited . . . and waited . . . and waited.

Milo shook his head. 'No,' he sighed. 'You're still the same Jack. No sign of Thud.'

Jack stopped scowling, unclenched his fists and looked miserable. 'I thought I'd done it,' he said unhappily.

'You did it once, you'll do it again!' said Meenu. She turned to Ava. 'Right, time to get your costume off and take a break before the next match.'

'Good idea,' said Ava. 'This mask is okay, but it's nicer when it's off.'

And she reached up to untie the straps at the back.

'Wait!' said Meenu. She went to the window and pulled the curtain shut. 'There!' she said. 'Just in case anyone's peering in through the windows. Now you can take your mask off.'

Outside the window and the now-closed curtain, Lord Veto let out a growl.

'Curses!' he said. 'Put me down, Warg!'

The orc bent down and let Lord Veto slide from his shoulders to the ground.

'No luck, my Lord?'

'No, they closed the curtain just as she was about to take her mask off!'

'There is a rumour, sir,' said Warg, 'that the Masked Avenger may actually be Princess Ava of Weevil.'

'What makes you say that?' demanded Lord Veto.

'Well, it's noticeable that the Masked Avenger only wrestles at tournaments when Princess Ava comes to watch. And no one can remember the Princess being in the audience when the Masked Avenger is actually wrestling.'

'Stuff and nonsense!' snapped Lord Veto. 'Poppycock, Warg! First, the Princess is a royal person. Someone like that, a true royal, would never lower herself to appear in public in a wrestling ring! And second: Princess Ava is the most girly girl I've ever seen. All curls and frills and things. The exact *opposite* of what a wrestler is.'

'If you say so, my Lord.'

'I do say so! No, the Masked Avenger is some mystery person, and I intend to find out who.' Then the sly smile appeared on his face again.

'But in the meantime, I've just learnt something as important. It turns out that that fantastic Wrestling Troll, Thud, is actually my puny former kitchen boy!' He smiled and punched his fists together with glee. 'If I could get Thud to join my stable of wrestlers, I could earn an absolute fortune from him! I'd be rich!'

'You're already rich, my Lord,' said Warg.

'I'd be even richer!' snapped Veto.

Warg looked doubtful.

'I don't think he'll join you, my Lord. He doesn't like you.'

'Oh, but he will,' smiled Lord Veto.

CHAPTER 3

Princess Ava and Meenu walked across the field to where their caravan was parked, not far from the WWT caravan.

'Let me guess,' said Ava. 'You saw someone peering in that window.'

'Yes,' said Meenu. 'Only I didn't see who it was.'

'I can tell you,' said a small sparrow, flying down and landing beside them, before turning into Blaze the Phoenix. 'It was Lord Veto and his Chief Orc, Warg.'

'How do you know?'

'I saw a movement outside the window, so I changed into a mouse and slipped out through a tiny hole in the wall to take a look.'

'I wondered where you'd vanished to!' said Meenu.

'Lord Veto is determined to find out the true identity of the Masked Avenger,' said Blaze.

'Oh is he?' Ava grinned. 'Well, maybe we can have a bit of fun with that!'

'He also found out that Jack can turn into Thud,' Blaze added.

'Hmm, that's not so funny,' said Ava thoughtfully. 'We'll have to be careful. Lord Veto is the sneakiest person there is. There's no knowing what he might do now he knows that.'

Jack lifted the lid of the outside compartment at the back of the caravan where Big Rock's wrestling equipment was kept. Robin complained that it added a lot of weight to the caravan, and he was the one who had to pull it along. But Jack pointed out that without all that equipment, Big Rock wouldn't be as good a wrestler as he was, so wouldn't be in demand by wrestling promoters, and they wouldn't get to go to so many interesting places.

'Good,' snorted Robin. 'Maybe I could get some rest. After all, I'm not as young as I used to be!'

But Jack knew the old horse didn't mean it. Robin enjoyed the travels with the gang as much as any of them.

Jack was sorting through the collection of rocks and stones that Big Rock also kept in the compartment, when he heard a voice behind him murmur:

'Why, it's Jack!'

Jack spun round and came face to face with Lord Veto. Immediately he growled, 'Get away from me!'

Lord Veto stopped and looked apologetic.

'I'm sorry if I startled you,' he said. 'I just want to apologise.'

Jack frowned and looked at Lord Veto suspiciously. 'What for?' he asked.

'For everything,' said Lord Veto. 'But especially for the way I treated you in the past. I was cruel to you, Jack. Not deliberately . . .'

'Yes, you were,' snapped Jack.

'I know it may have seemed that way at the time, but the truth is . . . I was thoughtless. Uncaring. Selfish. I realise that now. I was especially wrong to ban you from going to the wrestling tournament the way I did. I hadn't realised how much wrestling meant to you. But now I do. And I want to make it up to you.'

Jack looked at Lord Veto warily. He'd never seen Veto like this before.

Jack had worked in the kitchens at Veto Castle since he was a very small child, until Lord Veto kicked him out just before his tenth birthday. He had no memories of a time before he'd been at Veto Castle. His young life as a kitchen boy had been awful: he'd only had a basket to sleep in, and he'd lived on scraps of food. In all that time he'd never known Lord Veto be anything other than cruel and harsh, and he'd never said 'sorry' to *anyone*.

What was going on? Jack was sure that Lord Veto was up to some sneaky trick . . . but what?

'When you say you'd like to make it up to me . . .' said Jack warily. 'How?'

'I'd like to offer you the job of becoming chief trainer with my team of wrestlers. You will be paid very highly, as well as having the most luxurious apartment at Veto Castle. This is my way of saying "sorry", Jack. And also because I recognise the great things you've done with Big Rock. You are a top-class wrestling trainer!'

'Assistant trainer,' Jack corrected him.

Lord Veto gave a sigh. 'Yes, well, that may be true at the moment. But everyone knows that it is you, and not Milo, who has made Big Rock the great Wrestling Troll he is! Wherever I go, all the wrestling managers I meet talk about you, Jack, as the great trainer behind Big Rock, not Milo.' He looked sad as he added, 'I'm not saying that Milo is holding you back on purpose, because he's jealous of you . . .'

'Good!' snapped Jack.

'. . . but that's what other people are saying. Other trainers.'

'Well, they're wrong!' said Jack. 'Milo is a good trainer and manager. He was taking care of Big Rock before I joined them.'

'Yes, but *since* you've joined them look how much more famous Big Rock has become.'

Jack shook his head. 'No,' he said.

Lord Veto put on an appealing look. 'Jack, I know you feel you have no reason to trust me, but I want to prove to you that I've changed. I will give you a written contract with everything in it that I've just said: the job of chief trainer with my team of wrestlers, top rate of pay, and the most luxurious apartment at Veto Castle.'

Jack regarded Veto suspiciously.

'What about my friends?' he asked. 'Where would they fit into this?'

Lord Veto gave a sigh and shrugged. 'I'm afraid they're not included in my offer. It's you that I want, Jack. Your skill.'

Again, Jack shook his head. 'We can't be split up,' he said. 'We're a family.'

'Are you sure of that?' murmured Lord Veto.

Jack frowned. 'What do you mean?' he demanded.

'Well, how much do you trust Milo?' asked Veto.

'Completely,' said Jack firmly. 'We all look after one another.'

'Except for Milo, who looks after himself,' said Lord Veto.

'How dare you!' snapped Jack.

Lord Veto shook his head.

'You are so gullible, Jack. You and Big Rock. And that stupid horse.'

'We are friends! We trust one another. But someone like you wouldn't understand that.'

'On the contrary, Jack. I understand about "trust" only too well. For example, how much does Milo pay you?'

'It doesn't work like that,' retorted Jack. 'We share any money that comes in as a group, equally.'

'And who collects the money after a tournament?'

'Milo, of course. He's the manager.'

Lord Veto chuckled. 'And I suppose Milo tells you all how much he's collected.' And he laughed again.

'What's so funny?' demanded Jack.

'I know for a fact that Milo has a secret account at a money-house where he keeps a *lot* of money. He's been cheating you. All of you.'

'That's a lie!'

'Perhaps you'd like to see the proof of Milo's secret money account?'

'No!' Jack shouted angrily.

'What's going on?' asked a voice.

Jack and Lord Veto turned, and saw that Milo, Big Rock and Robin had appeared.

'Nothing!' snapped Jack, with a glare at Veto. 'Lord Veto was just going.'

'Yes, I am,' said Veto, nodding. He turned back to Jack. 'But bear in mind what I said. My offer still stands. I'll leave you to think about it.'

And with that, he walked off.

Jack looked after him and scowled. 'I don't trust him,' he said. 'Where's Blaze? We ought to get Blaze to change shape and follow him and find out what he's up to.'

'Blaze is with Ava and Meenu,' said Milo. 'Something to do with Lord Veto and his dirty tricks.' He gestured after the departing Veto. 'So what was all that about? You sounded really angry, shouting at him.'

'I am angry,' said Jack.

'Why, what did he say?' asked Robin.

'He offered me a job,' said Jack. 'Chief trainer with his team of wrestlers, top rate of pay and the most luxurious apartment at Veto Castle.'

'Yes,' nodded Robin. 'I can see how that sort of thing would make you angry.' And he gave a snort of a laugh.

'Good job offer,' said Big Rock. 'What you say?'

'What do you think I said?' demanded Jack indignantly. 'No, of course!'

'I also heard him say something about a secret money account,' said Robin. 'Just before you shouted at him.'

'Yes, well, that was something else,' said Jack awkwardly. He hesitated. 'He said that Milo had a secret account at a money-house. He suggested that you were keeping money from us.'

'*What?*' exclaimed Milo. He glared in the direction Lord Veto had gone. 'Why, the dirty, lying . . .'

'That's what I told him,' said Jack. 'That's why I shouted at him when he said he'd show me proof of your secret money-house account.'

'What proof?' asked Robin, intrigued.

'I don't know! I didn't give him a chance to say any more. That's when I shouted at him, and then you lot arrived.'

'There isn't any sort of proof because I haven't got a secret money account!' exploded Milo.

'Don't worry, we know that,' said Jack. 'He's just being sneaky, because he wants me to leave Waldo's Wrestling Trolls and join him. But it's not going to happen!'

CHAPTER 4

Princess Ava, dressed in her Masked Avenger costume, entered her caravan. Behind her came a tiny grey mouse, which turned into Blaze the Phoenix as soon as the caravan door was shut.

'I really don't like being a mouse,' complained Blaze. 'There was a cat following me right across the field, and there was an owl in the tree outside which woke up just now and gave me a really nasty look.'

'It won't be for much longer,' said Ava. 'Just as soon as we've played this trick on Lord Veto. You're sure he was following me?'

Blaze nodded.

'Yes, he was dodging from tree to tree, and hiding behind bushes. He should be arriving outside the caravan about now.'

The door to the small toilet opened and out came Meenu, dressed in Princess Ava's spare wrestling costume and wearing her spare mask.

'How do I look?' she asked.

'Great!' said Ava.

'The problem will be getting rid of Lord Veto after he's seen me,' said Meenu. 'We don't want him hanging around watching through the window for too long. You've got

another wrestling match coming up.'

'Don't worry,' grinned Ava. 'Leave that to Blaze. He's going to handle it.'

And with that Ava stepped into the toilet and pulled the door shut.

'The mouse again,' groaned Blaze. And with a sigh the phoenix burst into a bright flame and disappeared, to be replaced by the small grey mouse, which scampered towards the door and out through a small crack.

Outside the caravan, Lord Veto climbed up on one of the caravan wheels and clung onto a wooden ledge and peered in. Yes, there was the Masked Avenger!

As Lord Veto watched, the Masked Avenger took off her cloak and hung it up, and then she reached behind her head and unclipped the straps that held her mask in place. *Clip! Clip!* The mask came off to reveal . . .

'Meenu!' breathed Lord Veto.

He heard a squeak just below him, and looked down.

A small grey mouse had climbed up the wheel and was sitting on the toe of his shoe.

'Get off!' growled Lord Veto, and went to kick the mouse away; but before he could, the mouse ran up the inside of his trouser leg.

'*Aaaargh!*' yelled Lord Veto, and he fell off the wheel and landed with a thud on the grass.

'No!' he moaned as he felt the mouse run up his leg, and then run around inside his clothes, moving all over, tickling him with its whiskers and scratching his skin with its tiny paws.

'Get off!' he howled, and he rolled over and over, trying to squash the mouse, but the mouse carried on darting around inside his clothes.

Lord Veto leapt to his feet and ran, calling out, 'Warg! Help! Warg! Save me!'

The mouse slipped out of Lord Veto's trousers back onto the grass, and watched Veto run across the field, slapping his clothes as he went.

Lord Veto hid behind a bush in a state of undress, while Warg held up his trousers and shook them firmly.

'There's no mouse in here, my Lord,' said the orc.

'Are you sure?' demanded Lord Veto. 'It was only a small mouse. A sneaky one. It could be hiding in a fold or something.'

'Definitely no mouse,' said Warg.

He handed the trousers back to Lord Veto, who pulled them on and then stepped out from the cover of the bush.

'It doesn't matter,' said Lord Veto triumphantly. 'I saw enough. The Masked Avenger is Meenu!'

Warg looked doubtful.

'But that can't be so, my Lord,' he said.

'Why not?'

'Because whenever the Masked Avenger wrestles, Meenu is in her corner. I've seen her.'

'But I saw her face when she took her mask off! I tell you it was that girl, Meenu!' And then a light seemed to click on behind his eyes. 'Great shimmering toenails! I know how they do it!' he said triumphantly.

'How, my Lord?' asked Warg.

'Twins!' exclaimed Veto.

'Twins?'

'Meenu obviously has a twin sister! And that's why the Masked Avenger's so good, because they take turns to be her. That way one of them is always fresh enough for the match.' He shook his head in admiration. 'It's brilliant! It's worthy of a criminal super-genius.'

Warg looked doubtful. 'Are you sure, my Lord? You don't think it's more likely that Princess Ava –'

'Nonsense! Poppycock! Stuff and hoo-ha!

This has to be the answer. Meenu and her mystery twin sister are the Masked Avenger. And I shall catch them out, and force them to do what I want if they don't want the truth to come out.' He rubbed his hands together in glee. 'The Masked Avenger and Thud, added to my stable of wrestlers. This will be my biggest success!'

CHAPTER 5

'Trolls win! Orcs lose!' sang Big Rock cheerfully, and he added a fart noise to make clear his feelings about orcs.

Jack knelt beside the big troll in the caravan and finished sewing up one of the many holes in the troll's wrestling costume.

'You're going to need a new costume soon, Big Rock,' he said.

'This one good,' said Big Rock. 'Just keep patching it.'

'It's already got loads of patches on,' said Jack. 'In fact, it's got more patches than original costume.'

'Make it look good!' smiled Big Rock. 'Lots of different colours!'

'Right,' said Jack. 'Time to go and get the Masked Avenger and head for the Wrestling Hall. Here come the WWT Tag Team!'

'Great fun!' said Big Rock.

He was just about to head to the door when he stopped and pointed at something half-hidden beneath one of the bunks.

'What that?' he asked.

'What's what?' asked Jack.

Big Rock lifted a small leather bag from beneath the bunk.

'I've never seen it before,' said Jack. 'It's not mine. Perhaps it's Princess Ava's? Or Meenu's? They might have left it here and forgotten it.'

'I check,' said Big Rock.

He opened the bag and looked in.

'Not much here.' He shook the bag, and they heard the clink of metal. Big Rock turned the bag upside down, and two gold coins fell out on the table, along with a piece of paper.

Jack picked up the piece of paper and read out loud, '*The Dragon Money-house. Savings Account. Name: Milo the WWT Manager.*

Balance: one hundred gold coins.'

'Lot of money,' said Big Rock.

'It certainly is!' said Jack.

'Are you ready?' called Milo.

They looked around and saw that Milo and Princess Ava, wearing her Masked Avenger outfit, were peering into the caravan, with Meenu just behind them.

'Hurry up, Big Rock!' said Milo. 'You're due in the ring.'

'We look at money,' said Big Rock.

'What money?' asked Milo.

Milo, Ava and Meenu came in and looked at the two gold coins and the piece of paper. Ava picked up the piece of paper, read it, and whistled appreciatively.

'Wow, Milo!' she said. 'You're rich! A hundred gold coins!'

'What?' Milo snatched the piece of paper from the Princess and read it, then shook his head. 'This is rubbish!' he said. 'I don't have a deposit account at the Dragon Money-house!'

'Well, you do now,' said Jack.

'Jack's right.' Meenu nodded. 'As long as you've got this piece of paper you can go into any money-house and take this money out.'

'But it's not mine!' burst out Milo.

'Well, it's someone's,' said Jack thoughtfully.

'Someone called Milo the WWT Manager,' added Big Rock.

'It's not me!' shouted Milo. 'It's a . . . frame-up of some sort! Someone is trying to make you

think I've got a secret store of money.' Then he glared angrily at Jack and added, 'And it looks like they've succeeded!'

'No!' retorted Jack. 'How can you say that?'

'Because I can see it in your face,' snapped Milo. 'You think this money might really be mine.'

'No – I didn't think that!' said Jack. 'I was wondering whose it really was.'

'Liar!' shouted Milo.

'Wait a minute . . .' appealed Ava.

'No, I won't wait!' snapped Milo. 'I thought Jack was my friend, but here he is, accusing me –'

'I didn't accuse you,' snapped back Jack. 'And don't you dare say I did! And you can apologise to me for saying it!'

'*Me* apologise!' shouted Milo indignantly. 'I'm the one who ought to get an apology.'

'Guys, calm down,' urged Ava.

'Actually, Big Rock and Ava are due in the ring *now*,' said Meenu, gesturing at the caravan door. 'It's about to start.'

'Okay,' said Big Rock. 'Let's go beat orcs.'

And he headed out of the caravan, with Ava and Meenu following. Milo and Jack glared angrily at one another and then followed them. As they left the caravan, they met Robin, who asked, 'What was all that shouting about? I heard something about money.'

'Jack will tell you all about it,' stormed Milo. 'He thinks I'm a cheat and a crook who's been keeping money hidden from you all.' And he set off after Big Rock, Ava and Meenu.

'I never said that,' raged Jack. 'And you owe me an apology!'

Robin watched as Jack hurried to join the others.

'Out of curiosity, how much money are we talking about?' called the old horse.

CHAPTER 6

The Wrestling Hall was packed for the tag match: Big Rock and the Masked Avenger against two of Lord Veto's Wrestling Orcs, Bash and Bop. The rules of tag wrestling were simple: one wrestler from each team in the ring, and the other outside the ropes. When the wrestler in the ring wanted to take a break, they touched hands with – or tagged – the wrestler outside the ring, and the two changed places. At least, that was how it was supposed to work.

Both Big Rock and the Masked Avenger had wrestled orc tag teams before and knew that they often cheated, the one in the ring forcing their opponent towards their orc partner outside the ropes, and then both of them ganging up together, two against one.

Big Rock was starting, and he stood inside the ring as the two orcs climbed up. Bash, the guy orc, strode to the centre of the ring and strutted around, waving at the crowd, who cheered or booed, depending on which team they supported. Bop, the girl orc, stood on the ring ropes, ready for action.

Meenu stood in one corner just beneath the ring, holding the Masked Avenger's cloak. Further back in the hall, Lord Veto and Warg watched.

'See, my Lord,' whispered Warg. 'Meenu.'

Lord Veto shook his head.

'Her twin sister!' he said, smirking. 'The other one's in the ring.'

Jack and Milo stood by the exit, both glowering unhappily.

'Well, are you going to apologise?' demanded Milo.

'No!' snapped back Jack. '*I've* got nothing to apologise for! If there's any apology to be made it should come from you for saying what you said about me.'

'I only said what was true! You did look at me as if you didn't believe me.'

'That's rubbish. And if that's what you think of me, then I'm no longer your friend.'

'Well, if you feel like that, then maybe it's time we parted company!' snorted Milo.

Jack stopped and glared at Milo. Then he

said, 'Yes. Maybe it is.' And he turned and walked out of the Wrestling Hall.

Shocked by this action, Milo went to go after him, but then he stopped.

No, he told himself. It's up to Jack to say sorry.

In the ring, the bell had gone for the start of the bout. Bash dropped into a crouch, arms and claws held out towards Big Rock, then he retreated towards the ropes where Bop waited.

Big Rock advanced, but as he neared Bash, the orc suddenly dropped to the canvas and tripped him, at the same time grabbing him round the knees and pulling him forwards, off balance.

Big Rock tumbled, his upper body landing on the ropes. Immediately, Bop went into action. She grabbed Big Rock's arms and held him on the ropes, while Bash jumped on the troll's back.

'Referee!' shouted the Masked Avenger in protest. 'Foul!'

The referee ran to where the two orcs were both attacking Big Rock.

'Separate!' he ordered. 'Separate!'

But the two orcs ignored him, and while Bop held grimly onto Big Rock's arms, Bash lifted the troll's feet into the air, ready to hurl him through the ropes and out of the ring.

This was too much for the Masked Avenger. She vaulted over the ropes and pulled Bash backwards by the shoulders, then continued the move, throwing the orc over her shoulder so he landed with a ring-shaking crash in the centre.

Bop let out a cry of fury and leapt into the ring, hurling herself at the Masked Avenger, but Big Rock had seen her move. He grabbed the orc by one arm and twirled her around his body, then threw her into the corner post.

'Stop!' shouted the referee. 'Only two wrestlers at a time in the ring!'

'They started it!' protested the Masked Avenger.

'Yes, orcs cheat!' said Big Rock.

'I'm the referee!' he snapped. 'I'm the only one who can say if there's cheating going on, and I say . . . *Aaaargh!*'

Bash and Bop had picked up the referee and thrown him out of the ring. He crashed down on the area outside, narrowly missing Meenu and Milo.

'That is definitely not in the rules,' said Milo, helping the dazed referee to his feet.

In the ring, a battle was raging as Bash and Bop clawed and kicked at Big Rock and the Masked Avenger, using every sneaky trick the orcs could come up with – but Big Rock and the Avenger were holding their own.

The crowd roared, cheering on their own particular favourites, with shouts and chants of 'Orcs! Orcs!' and 'Big Rock and the Masked Avenger!' The noise in the hall was so loud that at first no one could hear the bell being rung. The referee clambered back into the ring, put a whistle to his lips and began to blow hard, the shrill blast gradually making the noise from the audience subside, and the four wrestlers disentangled themselves from one another and stepped back and regarded the referee.

The referee, furious, pointed at the two orcs.

'Throwing the referee out of the ring is the worst foul you can do!' he shouted. 'You are both disqualified!'

At this there was a huge roar from the audience, and Bash and Bop advanced menacingly on the referee, sparks coming from their claws as they clashed them together.

'And if you dare to touch me again, I'll ban you from all competitions!' shouted the referee.

Bash and Bop stopped and exchanged unhappy looks. With a last glare at Big Rock and the Masked Avenger, they ran back to their dressing room.

Even in defeat, the cheers of the orcs' supporters were ringing around the hall . . . But they were matched by the cheers for the victors as the referee announced: 'I declare the winners of this tag contest to be . . . Big Rock and the Masked Avenger!'

The champions climbed out of the ring, high-fiving everyone. Big Rock looked around, and then asked: 'Where's Jack?'

Milo shrugged. 'I don't know. He walked out.'

'Walked out?' said the Masked Avenger in surprise.

'Where?' asked Meenu.

Milo shrugged again. 'I think he might have gone back to the caravan,' he said.

'Okay, we go tell him we win!' beamed Big Rock. 'Beat orcs!'

And the big troll headed for the door.

Meenu looked at Milo suspiciously.

'What's going on?' she demanded.

'Nothing,' he said defensively.

And he set off after Big Rock and the Masked Avenger. Meenu frowned and went after them. Something was not right.

As they neared their caravans, they found Robin and Blaze heading towards them.

'What's going on?' demanded the old horse angrily.

'We win!' smiled Big Rock. 'Me and Masked Avenger beat Lord Veto's orcs!'

'I don't mean that! I mean, why has Jack packed his bags and gone?'

CHAPTER 7

They stared at the horse, shocked.

'Gone?'

Blaze nodded.

'We asked him where he was going, and why, and he just said, "Ask Milo" . . .'

They all turned to look at Milo.

'Well?' demanded Robin.

'We had a bit of a row,' said Milo awkwardly.

'I knew it!' said Meenu.

'Oh, you pair of idiots!' said Princess Ava. 'Was this about that money business?'

'Well, yes,' said Milo. 'He said . . . something . . . and I said . . .'

'Oh, you fool!' said Ava. 'It was obvious to anyone with half a brain that that piece of paper was a fake.'

'That's what I said . . .' said Milo defensively.

'You accused Jack of thinking badly of you,' said Meenu.

'Well . . . he did,' said Milo. 'He thought I'd stolen that money from him and Big Rock and Robin.'

'No, he didn't!' snapped Ava. 'Because, like I said, it was obvious to anyone with half a brain that that piece of paper was a fake, and Jack has got a good brain. He knew it was a fake!'

'Then why didn't he say so?'

'He did, but you weren't listening to him properly because you were too upset and more bothered about your hurt feelings!' said Ava. She groaned. 'What are we going to do?'

Lord Veto and Warg watched all this from behind the cover of a tree.

'It seems that Jack has left them, my Lord,' Warg said.

'Indeed!' Lord Veto beamed. 'My plan is working!'

'So, shall we go after Jack?'

Lord Veto shook his head. 'No, no. He'll come to me.'

Warg looked doubtful. 'But say he doesn't? Say he decides to go far, far away instead?'

'No, Warg. Trust me. I understand people. That is why I am rich and successful while you are just . . . an orc. We'll let Jack wander around for a bit, getting more and more miserable. When he's miserable enough, he'll think about how good my offer is.' He winked. 'It's always best to have the upper hand in any negotiations, Warg. That means *he* has to come to *me*, asking for a favour. Not the other way round.' He grinned. 'Anyway, at the moment I am about to put the other part of my plan into operation: getting the Masked Avenger onto my team.'

'How will you do that, my Lord?'

'Blackmail, Warg,' smiled Lord Veto. 'Blackmail and money.'

Jack sat on a large rock and looked at the road that wound onwards. Where would he go? He looked at his bag by his feet. All his worldly possessions were in there: a few clothes, and programmes from tournaments when Jack had been part of Big Rock's team . . . with Milo.

Now, that was all gone. He'd left them far behind when he left the caravan, and now he'd never see them again.

As these thoughts came to him, he felt tears

fill his eyes. Milo accusing him like that was so unfair! He'd thought he'd found friends for life when he'd joined up with Milo, Big Rock and Robin . . . but he'd been wrong. There was no such thing as 'friends for life'. Milo had shown him that by being so horrible to him.

I should have told Blaze I was going, he thought. Blaze has been my friend. He'll miss me. And Big Rock. And Robin. But I can't stay with them, not after Milo acted the hurtful way he did towards me.

He dropped his head and tears splashed down onto the ground at his feet.

I've never been so unhappy, he sighed to himself. Not even when my life was at its worst, working in Lord Veto's kitchens.

A flapping sound above him made him look up. Blaze swooped down from the sky and landed on the ground beside him.

'The others sent me to find you,' said Blaze.

'Well, you've found me,' said Jack, wiping his eyes. 'Now leave me alone.'

The phoenix looked at Jack for a while,

thoughtfully. Then he said, 'Sorry, I can't do that.' Blaze changed into a very large dragon and, rising into the air, wings flapping, he picked up Jack, hooked Jack's bag on his claws and flew off, soaring ever higher.

Then he flew even higher yet.

'Let me go!' shouted Jack.

'That's not a good idea,' said Blaze. 'You'd fall a very long way and hurt yourself.'

'If you're taking me back to Milo, it's a waste of time, because I'm not going to say sorry to him,' said Jack.

'That's up to you . . . but he wants to say sorry to you. That's why he sent me.'

Jack fell silent for a moment, then said, 'Did he really?'

'Yes. Now shut up and let me concentrate on flying.'

Milo, Princess Ava, Meenu, Big Rock and Robin stood in the field by their caravans and stared into the distance, scanning the sky.

'There's no sign of Blaze,' worried Milo.

'Jack can't have gone *that* far,' said Meenu.

'Maybe Blaze can't find him,' said Big Rock.

'Or maybe Jack doesn't want to come back,' said Robin.

Princess Ava heard a beating sound behind them and turned. 'Or maybe we're looking in the wrong direction.'

The others all turned and watched as the big dragon flew lower and then landed beside them, dropping Jack and his bag on the ground.

'Jack!' cried Milo delightedly, and he ran towards him. 'I'm sorry I said what I did, Jack. I didn't mean it.'

Jack got to his feet and put his arms around Milo and hugged him.

'I'm sorry for going off like that, Milo,' Jack said. 'And for saying the things I said to you.'

'Good,' said Ava. 'Now we've got that out of the way, can we get back to the important business of who did it, and what we're going to do to pay him back?'

'But we don't know who did it,' said Milo.

'Of course we do!' said Ava impatiently.

'Who's the person who's got something to gain by splitting up the gang? Who wanted Jack to leave Waldo's Wrestling Trolls and join him and his Wrestling Orcs? Who's the one person we know who's rich enough to be able to put a hundred gold coins into someone's money-house account?'

'Lord Veto,' said Meenu, Robin and Blaze together.

'Exactly!' said Ava. She glared accusingly at Jack and Milo. 'And you let him do it to you! You're a pair of idiots!'

'We ought to teach him a lesson,' said Meenu.

'Jack turn into Thud and throw Lord Veto around?' suggested Big Rock hopefully.

'Better than that,' said Meenu. 'Hit him where it hurts him most!'

'On his nose?' asked Robin.

'In his pocket!' said Ava. 'Money!'

CHAPTER 8

Meenu was folding the Masked Avenger's costumes and putting them neatly away when there was a knock at the caravan door.

'Yes?' she called.

The door opened and Lord Veto looked in.

'Good afternoon.' He smiled.

'What do you want?' demanded Meenu.

'Just a moment of your time,' said Lord Veto, and he stepped in. 'I wondered how you feel about *wrestling*?'

'How I feel about it?' said Meenu, puzzled. 'I like it. That's why I'm the Masked Avenger's costume designer and dresser.'

'And you are also very good friends with Princess Ava of Weevil, aren't you?' said Veto.

'Yes,' said Meenu. 'We've been friends for years, long before she became ruler of Weevil.'

'And you'd hate to do anything that might embarrass her,' said Veto. 'Especially with her being so very important. I mean, if it were discovered that a close friend of hers was a cheat, a liar and a fraud, it would make her position as ruler of Weevil very difficult. She might even have to abdicate and let someone else take over. After all, no one would trust a ruler who, in turn, trusted someone who was a liar and a fraud.'

'Are you calling me a liar and a fraud?' demanded Meenu angrily.

Veto didn't answer this. Instead, he smirked. Then, 'Who is the Masked Avenger?' he asked.

'That is a secret!' snapped Meenu.

'Is it?' murmured Veto. 'Well, what if I told you I know the secret?' He leant into Meenu and whispered menacingly, 'What if I told you that I know it's you and your twin sister? And that you take turns in being the Masked Avenger?'

'I'd say you were talking rubbish!' retorted Meenu.

'But what would the wrestling authorities say about it if I told them?' continued Veto. 'They'd ban the Masked Avenger from wrestling.' He snickered. 'And, as I say, once the truth got out, Princess Ava would be left in a very awkward position.'

Meenu fell silent for a moment, then she said, 'What if this stupid story was true? What do you plan to do about it?'

Lord Veto gave a shrug and a wink.

'Why, nothing!' he said. 'Provided the Masked Avenger joins my stable of wrestlers.'

'Yours?' asked Meenu.

Lord Veto smiled and produced a piece of paper. 'I have a contract right here,' he said, offering it to Meenu.

Meenu took it and read it aloud. '*I, Meenu, agree to wrestle for Lord Veto's Wrestlers, in partnership with my twin sister.*'

She shook her head. 'I can't sign this,' she said.

'Yes, you can,' said Veto. 'Or else, Princess Ava will suffer. And the Masked Avenger will be banned.'

Meenu fell silent. Then she said, 'There's no mention of money.'

Lord Veto smiled.

'Ah, money!' he said. 'I can offer you five gold coins. Providing you sign the contract, of course.'

'Non-refundable?' asked Meenu. 'I mean, I have to protect myself. Say I take the money

and sign this contract, and then you do something to break the contract – I'll have to give you the money back.'

'I won't break the contract,' said Lord Veto. 'I give you my word.'

Meenu shook her head. 'Your word is not worth a lot, Lord Veto,' she sniffed. She picked up a pen and wrote a few words on the contract.

'What are you writing?' asked Lord Veto suspiciously.

'I'll read it to you,' said Meenu. Aloud, she read out, '*I, Meenu, agree to wrestle for Lord Veto's Wrestlers, in partnership with my twin sister, for the sum of five gold coins. This money will be kept by Meenu even if the contract is broken for any reason.*'

'Agreed!' said Lord Veto.

'Let me have the money first,' said Meenu.

Lord Veto hesitated, then dug into his pocket and produced a handful of gold coins. He counted out five of them and gave them to Meenu.

'There,' he said. 'Now sign the contract.'

'I need to have a copy as well,' said Meenu.

'I've got another copy,' said Lord Veto, and he pulled a further copy of the contract from his pocket.

Meenu added her extra wording to that copy as well, then signed her name on both and gave one back to Lord Veto.

'There,' she said. 'I hope you're satisfied.'

Lord Veto smiled.

'Oh yes, I am very satisfied,' he said, beaming. 'Welcome to Lord Veto's stable of wrestlers, Masked Avenger.'

CHAPTER 9

Lord Veto was smiling and chuckling to himself as he neared the Wrestling Hall. Life was good! Business was booming! It almost made him feel like singing! Things couldn't be better! And his voice broke into a warbling:

> 'I am so happy!
> I am so clever!
> I will be rich for ever and ever.
> Now I have the Masked Avenger.
> And soon I'll have Thud!
> Oh, clever me!'

Then he heard Warg's voice calling, 'Lord Veto! Lord Veto!'

The Chief Orc sounded panicky. Lord Veto

turned and saw Warg running as fast as he could towards him, waving his arms, then skidding to a halt beside him.

'What is it?' demanded Lord Veto.

'The Masked Avenger . . .' panted Warg, out of breath.

'Signed and sealed!' grinned Lord Veto, and he produced the contract with a flourish and thrust it under the orc's nose. 'What did I tell you? Blackmail and money! It never fails!'

The orc scanned the contract, and then shook his head. 'This contract is null and void,' he said. 'It's worthless.'

'What do you mean?' demanded Lord Veto indignantly. 'She's signed it! That's her signature! It's legal!'

Warg shook his head.

'This says *in partnership with my twin sister . . .*'

'Of course it does! That's the whole point! I need both sisters!'

'Meenu doesn't have a twin sister,' said Warg. 'She doesn't have a sister at all. Or a brother.

Or any other relatives. Not even a cousin.'

'What?' said Veto, shocked. 'Are you sure?'

'Certain, my Lord. I checked and double-checked.'

'Then, if she isn't the Masked Avenger, who is?'

'As I mentioned, my Lord . . .' began Warg hesitantly.

'If you're going to start again with that nonsense about it being Princess Ava, forget it!' snorted Lord Veto. 'As I said before, she is royal and a very girly girl! It is obviously not her!'

'No, my Lord,' nodded Warg.

'And right now we have a more important issue to deal with. I've just given that girl five gold coins! I'll get those back to start with.'

'You can't, my Lord,' said Warg.

'Of course I can!' snorted Veto. 'She lied to me! She pretended to have a twin sister, when she hasn't. That means she's broken the contract, so I get my money back.'

Warg pointed a claw at the words that Meenu

had added to the contract and read them aloud: '*This money will be kept by Meenu even if the contract is broken for any reason.*' He sighed. 'My Lord, you've been conned.'

'*What?*' said Lord Veto. He stared at the contract in his hand, and then began tearing the paper into shreds.

'There is no contract!' he raged. 'I'll destroy it!'

'Unless she has a copy,' said Warg.

Lord Veto stopped and a look of pain passed over his face.

'They've cheated me! I've just lost five gold coins! I bet they were all in on it! Meenu, Milo, Robin . . .'

A look of grim and evil determination replaced his look of pain. 'Just you wait! I'll have my own back on them! Once that miserable former kitchen boy of mine crawls back to me, begging for me to take him on . . .' He gave an evil smile. 'Not that I'll honour my promise, of course. Chief trainer! I don't want him as a trainer. I want him as Thud the Wrestling Troll!'

'Are you sure he'll come to you, my Lord?' asked Warg.

'Yes! The boy loves wrestling, and now he's left Milo and his stupid Waldo's Wrestling Trolls, my wrestling stable is the only game left open to him!'

The orc's beak fell open and his eyes widened in surprise as he spotted something over Lord Veto's shoulder.

'My Lord!' said Warg, stunned. 'I think you may be right!'

Lord Veto turned and saw the small figure of Jack heading towards them.

'See, Warg! What did I tell you? I know how people work!'

He smiled as Jack neared.

'Jack!' he said. 'It's good to see you again. Even though you were obviously unhappy at our last encounter –'

'I have a question, Lord Veto,' said Jack curtly, cutting him off.

'Yes?' asked Lord Veto.

'Before, you were talking about Milo taking

money from us and hiding it in a money-house account.'

'Yes?' said Lord Veto again, warily this time.

'Well, we found a bag in our caravan, containing two gold coins and a piece of paper stating there was a money-house account with a hundred gold coins in it.'

'And was there a name on this piece of paper?' asked Lord Veto.

'Yes,' said Jack. 'Milo, Manager of WWT.'

'Oh dear!' said Lord Veto, looking sorrowful. 'This must have come as a great shock to you!'

'It did.' Jack nodded.

'This suggests that the stories I heard about Milo were true.' He shook his head. 'Terrible! Who'd have thought someone claiming to be your friend could have done such a thing!'

'So what it states on this piece of paper is right?' asked Jack. 'It's got Milo's name on it and says he's got a hundred gold coins in the Dragon Money-house. So that really is his money?'

'I'm afraid so,' sighed Lord Veto unhappily.

'Oh Jack, what can I do to help you get over finding out this terrible thing?'

'Nothing!' said Jack with a cheerful smile.

'What?' Lord Veto demanded, bewildered.

'Well, if it's his money, he can take it out of the money-house. It's exactly the amount that Princess Ava needs to repair the damage that terrible storm did. The people of Weevil will be so grateful!'

'*What?*' squawked Lord Veto. 'But . . . he can't!'

'Why not?' asked Jack.

'Because . . . Because . . .' Lord Veto spluttered. 'Because he can't!'

'But you just said he can.'

'Yes, but . . .'

'Anyway, it doesn't matter. Milo has gone with the others to the money-house to take his money out. All one hundred gold coins of it.'

'But that's my money!' screeched Lord Veto.

'*Your* money?' said Jack in a surprised voice. 'But I thought you said –'

'Forget what I said!' howled Lord Veto.

'Warg! Tie this boy up and throw him in my carriage. Then round up my Wrestling Orcs and get us to the Dragon Money-house. We have to stop Milo getting that money out!'

CHAPTER 10

Jack bounced around inside the carriage as it rattled along at frantic speed through the cobbled streets of the small town. He wriggled and struggled, trying to get out of the ropes that bound him, but it was no use – the knots had been tied too tightly. His one consolation was that Veto and his orcs would arrive too late; by now Milo should have already emptied the money-house account.

One hundred gold coins! Plus the five gold coins that Lord Veto gave Meenu; plus the two gold coins Lord Veto had slipped inside the leather bag he'd left in their caravan to try and frame Milo; plus the winnings of Big Rock and the Masked Avenger from their bouts – that would give a total of 110 gold coins, exactly the sum needed to repair the storm damage at Weevil. Providing Milo had already got hold of the money, of course.

But Jack didn't see why that shouldn't be the case. He'd waited until Milo and the others were just about to set off for the money-house before going to see Lord Veto, to give them a head-start. He'd been wary about telling Lord Veto, but Milo and Princess Ava had insisted, saying it was 'the honest thing to do'.

'We don't want him accusing Milo of theft,' said Princess Ava. 'We need him to say that the money *is* Milo's to take out.'

Lord Veto sat inside the carriage, squashed between Warg and another large orc, a vengeful look on his face, his feet resting on Jack's trussed-up body. More orcs were balanced on the roof of the carriage, holding on grimly as it raced through the streets. Jack could hear the one at the reins shouting at the horses, urging them to go faster.

'Have you got that potion, Warg?' asked Veto.

'Yes, my Lord.' He took a bottle out of his pocket.

Potion? thought Jack. For what?

Lord Veto saw Jack's puzzled expression and gave an evil smile. 'I know all about your pet phoenix, kitchen boy! That it can change shape and turn into other animals. Well, this stuff will put a stop to that! One squirt, and your pet will be useless. Not only will it not be able to change shape, but if it does that trick of setting fire to itself and turning into ashes, this time it won't be coming back! It'll be burnt and gone for ever!'

He gave a cackling laugh.

'No,' begged Jack. 'Please, leave Blaze alone!'

There was a screeching of brakes and a clattering of hooves as the carriage shuddered to a halt.

'We're here, my Lord!' shouted Warg.

Lord Veto threw open the door and trod painfully on Jack as he jumped out of the carriage.

'What shall we do with the boy?' asked one of the orcs, pointing at Jack.

'Throw him out!' snapped Lord Veto. 'I never want to see him again!'

The orcs picked Jack up and threw him out, and he landed on the pavement with a thud. Again, he wriggled and struggled to get the ropes off, but it was no use.

'There they are!' shouted Warg. 'We've got here before them, my Lord!'

Jack looked along the street and was shocked to see Milo, Big Rock, Meenu, Princess Ava (in her Masked Avenger costume) and Robin walking *towards* the money-house, with Blaze flying overhead! They should have taken the money out already! What had happened to delay them?

'Milo,' he shouted desperately. 'Look out! Blaze, keep away!'

By now Warg and the orcs – Jack counted ten of them, all fierce Wrestling Orcs – had blocked the entrance to the building that had the words *Dragon Money-house* over its doorway.

'Warg, stop them going in! And get that piece of paper off Milo!' shouted Lord Veto. He looked down at Jack and sneered. 'Without that piece of paper, that money stays where it is . . . until *I* take it out!'

Jack writhed around, desperately trying to turn into Thud.

'You're a crook, Lord Veto,' Jack shouted. 'You're a cheat and a liar!'

'Yes!' Lord Veto proudly smiled. 'And I'm good at it!'

Jack looked and saw that a pitched battle was taking place as Big Rock, holding Milo under one arm, was trying to force his way through the crowd of orcs into the money-house. Robin and the Masked Avenger were

joining in, punching and – in the case of Robin – kicking, while Meenu leapt on the orcs who were clambering all over Big Rock.

Please, let me change into Thud! begged Jack, and he shut his eyes and willed himself to turn into the giant troll, thinking troll thoughts, bringing troll images into his mind.

Thud! Thud! Thud! he urged himself . . . and then he felt a rocky film of transparent quartz begin to form over his eyes and a shudder passed through him. He felt his bones and muscles get bigger, stronger, straining against the ropes . . . It was happening! He was turning into Thud!

And then . . . it stopped. The quartz film over his eyes faded and he opened his eyes to see that he was still Jack: small, frail, thin Jack, still tied up tightly.

'No!' he groaned.

The orcs were winning, he could see that. Big Rock was now holding Milo high above his head, keeping the manager away from the clutching claws of the orcs, who were climbing up the big troll, closing in on him.

Then Jack saw Blaze swoop down from above.

'No, Blaze!'

The phoenix ignored Jack and landed on a pair of orcs, changing, in a burst of flames, from the phoenix into a dragon, the dragon's claws plucking the orcs off Big Rock.

'Do it, Warg!' shouted Lord Veto. 'Use the potion!'

Jack struggled frantically as he saw Warg about to take the top off the bottle of liquid. Tears of anger and desperation filled his eyes. Not normal tears, but a sort of crystal-like tears.

'*GRAAARRRRR!*'

The ropes split apart and fell away from Thud the Giant Wrestling Troll as he leapt up from the pavement.

Warg looked dumbfounded as the huge creature reached out and snatched the bottle from his hand, then grabbed Warg and threw him into the road.

The other orcs had turned in surprise at the roaring sound, and now backed away nervously.

Thud turned around to face Lord Veto, a terrifying scowl on the huge troll's face.

'*GRAAAARRRR!*' he roared.

Lord Veto blanched and backed away. He ran to the carriage, leapt into the driving seat and grabbed the reins.

'Go!' he shouted at the horses. Immediately they raced off, their hooves clattering on the cobbles.

'Wait, my Lord!' yelled Warg. He and the other orcs began to chase after the departing carriage.

Meenu looked at Thud as the huge troll shivered, and then began to grow smaller . . . and smaller . . .

'Wow, Jack!' she said. 'That was incredible!'

'What's in the bottle?' asked Robin, curiously.

'It's dangerous,' said Jack. 'It could have finished off Blaze for ever.'

'Give it to me,' said the Masked Avenger, taking the bottle from Jack and putting it in her pocket. 'I'll take it back to Weevil and let the Royal Scientist have a look at it, to try and find out what it is. If it's as dangerous as you say, we need to come up with an antidote.'

Jack looked at Milo, exasperated, and demanded, 'What took you so long to get here?'

'I couldn't find the piece of paper!' admitted Milo, embarrassed. 'Then I remembered, I'd got so angry that I'd screwed it up and thrown it away.'

'And it took us ages to find it,' grumbled Robin.

'But got it now,' beamed Big Rock. 'Let's get money!'

The two caravans trundled along the road, one behind the other, until they came to a fork. Princess Ava pulled her horse to a halt.

'This is where we part company!' she called. 'Thanks for the money. I still feel bad about taking it.'

'Don't!' Milo smiled. 'It will help a lot of people.'

'Yes, but Big Rock needs a new costume.'

'I like this costume,' said Big Rock obstinately.

'I'll tell you what; I'll make you a new one,' offered Meenu.

'Great!' said Milo. 'What do you say, Big Rock?'

Big Rock looked doubtful. 'I like this one.'

'I know, but don't say no until you've seen it,' said Meenu. She waved goodbye as Ava flicked the reins and their caravan headed off down the right-hand fork towards Weevil.

'I assume we're taking the other road?' said Robin gloomily.

'Yes,' said Milo.

'It's uphill,' pointed out Robin.

'Yes, but there's a great wrestling tournament at a town a few miles along it.'

'How long is a few miles?' asked Robin suspiciously.

'Er . . . about twenty.'

'Twenty miles?'

'Yes.'

'And uphill?'

'Not the *whole* way,' said Milo. 'The last bit goes downhill.'

'How long is the last bit?' asked Robin.

'Er . . . about half a mile,' admitted Milo.

Robin sighed. 'Oh well,' he said. 'But no singing!' he warned sternly.

And he headed off down the left-hand fork.

As the caravan creaked its way uphill, Jack whispered to Milo, 'I think a song might help Robin get into a rhythm, especially as going uphill is such hard work.'

'Do you think so?' Milo whispered back.

'Well, if he doesn't like it, I'm sure he'll say so,' replied Jack. And he began:

> 'Wrestling Trolls.
> Tum-di-dum!'

Then he stopped and waited.

Robin stopped.

'He doesn't like it,' whispered Milo.

'Look!' snorted the old horse. 'If you start something, at least finish it. It's very distracting having something unfinished in your head!'

'Okay,' nodded Jack. And he resumed singing:

'Wrestling Trolls.
Tum-di-dum!
Wrestling Trolls.
Tum-di-dum!'

Milo, Big Rock and Blaze added their voices, and soon even Robin was joining in as they all sang:

'Wrestling Trolls.
Tum-di-dum!
Wrestling Trolls.
Tum-di-dum!'

HOT KEY BOOKS

Thank you for choosing a Hot Key book.

If you want to know more about our authors and what we publish, you can find us online.

You can start at our website

www.hotkeybooks.com

And you can also find us on:

We hope to see you soon!

Lovereading4kids reader reviews of
Wrestling Trolls Match 1: Big Rock and the Masked Avenger
by Jim Eldridge

'I really like Wrestling Trolls. I really like Robin the horse because he talks, Big Rock because he's nice, Jack because he saves Princess Ava, and Princess Ava because she wrestles!'

Richie, age 7

'Wrestling Trolls is an action-packed book with awesome wrestling moves. The characters are clever and funny. I loved the story and can't wait to read the next instalment.'

Jacob, age 9

'The story had funny parts, action and good characters. Some of my favourite parts were Jack turning into a wrestling troll and I liked Robin the horse because he was grumpy and helpful.'

Jack, age 8

'It was brilliant! I liked how Jack changed into Thud - I won't tell you what Thud is so I don't give away the story . . . I really liked the song and keep singing it.'

George, age 7

'Wrestling Trolls is exciting because it is full of action. This book is fantastic if you like lots of wrestling and people being rescued from bad guys.'

Thomas, age 7

'I give it 10/10 even though I don't like wrestling, because I liked the story!'

Alexander, age 8